THE DISAPPEARANCE

also by ilan stavans

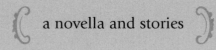

a novella and stories

the disappearance

ILAN STAVANS

TRIQUARTERLY BOOKS
NORTHWESTERN UNIVERSITY PRESS
EVANSTON, ILLINOIS

TriQuarterly Books
Northwestern University Press
www.nupress.northwestern.edu

Printed in the United States of America

10   9   8   7   6   5   4   3   2   1

ISBN 0-8101-2374-6

Library of Congress Cataloging-in-Publication Data

Stavans, Ilan.
    The disappearance : a novella and stories / Ilan Stavans.
        p. cm.
    Contents: The disappearance — Morirse está en hebreo — Xerox man.
    ISBN 0-8101-2374-6 (alk. paper)
    1. Silence—Fiction. I. Title.
PS3619.T385D57 2006
813.54—dc22

                                                    2006008898

♾ The paper used in this publication meets the
minimum requirements of the American National
Standard for Information Sciences—Permanence of
Paper for Printed Library Materials, ANSI Z39.48-1992.

The art of losing isn't hard to master;
so many things seem filled with the intent
to be lost . . .

Elizabeth Bishop, "One Art"

contents

preface

The three stories in this volume are concerned, in one way or another, with silence—both earthly and divine. There is another element that unites them: every one of the plots came to me from another source. My job, thus, has been rather simple: to falsify them until they became sheer fiction. "The Disappearance," my favorite, emerged in 2004 at the request of Jennifer Rosner—a digression on what she called "The Messy Self." It is inspired by the tortured case of a prominent actor, Jules Croiset, in the Low Countries that scandalized the world in 1988. I first read about it in the *New York Times*. For years I saved the news clipping, waiting for a moment to appropriate the tale. The dates are all accurate, as is the spirit of the protagonist's staged exit and reentrance. I've only dabbled with the proper names, the protagonist's psychological upbringing, and the rationale behind his escape.

"Morirse está en hebreo," a period drama, made primarily of dialogue and inspired by a Japanese work of Juzo

Itami's, is by far the longest. (The publisher is implausibly calling it, for marketing reasons, a novella.) The Mexican filmmaker Alejandro Springall and I devised its foundation during a three-hour conversation at a Holiday Inn. It is about the departure, physical and spiritual, of an authority figure, a Jewish entrepreneur in Mexico, as the country's fateful presidential elections of 2000 are taking place. My intention was to play the macrocosms and microcosms against each other. Improbably, a relative of mine, of exactly the same age as Moishe Tartakovsky, died the protagonist's same death: massive, instantaneous, and unexpected, also on a Friday morning. In addition, family members thought they knew the relative well. Nevertheless, it became evident during the shivah, as people recreated their impressions of the deceased, that there were more selves inside one body than seeds in an orange. By the time the story was finished, Springall was already turning it into a feature film (with my father, Abraham Stavans, in the cast).

"Xerox Man" was written while I lived in London. It was commissioned by BBC radio and aired in 1999. As stated in the opening paragraph, the essentials come from an article I read in *Harper's* a few years prior about a thief of antiquarian books. Again, I saved the material. Years later, I mentioned it to an editor. "Why don't you use it to explore the concept of originality?" he asked. Reuben Staflovitch's physical attributes I borrowed from an autistic friend, now deceased, I met in Buenos Aires. He often spoke in short, epigrammatic captions he found in books. I remember one from Graham Greene: "It isn't easy for a person to remain a pleasant human being: both success and failure are usually of a crippling kind." I've attempted to infuse the dialogue in the story with his spirit.

Over the years, I've been in pursuit of what Flaubert, in his correspondence with Sainte-Beuve, called *"le mot juste."* Writing isn't about finding any words to express myself but about finding the right words. The distinction is crucial. There is a plethora of examples available in the local bookstore—good ideas that have been poorly articulated. And how does one find the "right" word? There is no formula, but it is advisable to start by thinking clear thoughts. Once those thoughts have been fully understood, the task is to purge fake embellishments from the language. After all, language is the fabric we use to dress up thoughts. Finding the right dress is a matter of style, for sure, but also of instinct. Mark Twain put it best: "The difference between any word and the 'right' word is the difference between the lightning bug and the lightning."

I'm allergic to verbal excess. "What can be said at all can be said clearly," Ludwig Wittgenstein believed, "and whereof one cannot speak thereof one must be silent." In his *Philosophical Investigations,* he also claimed that "language is a labyrinth of paths. You approach from one side and know your way about; you approach the same place from another side and no longer know your way about." Finding *le mot juste* means rejecting needless adjectives. It means rejecting the practice of looting the thesaurus of synonyms. Complex ideas can be expressed with simplicity. Furthermore, I'm convinced that every argument, every plot, have an exact way of coming to life, of being articulated. This conviction of mine may be the result of my love affair with dictionaries. It may be a reaction to the obtuseness of academia, where language conceals rather than reveals meaning. And it may be the result of the translingual journey I've embarked upon: from Spanish and Yiddish and Hebrew into English. Other tongue-snatchers— Joseph Conrad, Vladimir Nabokov, Samuel Beckett— have also been obsessed with finding the right word. All writers are aware that every word they utter, every sentence they compose, are tests. For the tongue-snatcher, the test is twice as challenging: it isn't only a matter of stating things clearly but of doing so in someone else's territory.

A final caveat: I abhor the recent practice in English-language publishing of translating all foreign terms, assuming that the average monolingual reader is incapable of going beyond his intellectual confines. Montaigne, Erasmus of Rotterdam, and Robert Burton, to name but three "polyphonists," were not held hostage to the same superstition. Their work is filled with portions delivered in more recondite tongues than their own. In the pages that follow, I've left a number of "alien" expressions untranslated. My decision isn't about exoticism, as some critics have put it, but about the multilayered nature of speech in a fractured universe like ours.

Honest gentleman, I know not your breeding.

Henry IV, Part II, Act V

{ *the disappearance* }

FOR VERÓNICA ALBIN

I wonder if stomach cancer is one of the prices one might pay for gluttony, for that is what killed Maarten Soëtendrop at the age of seventy-one. It was my old friend, Yosee Strigler, who wrote informing me of the death of the corpulent, legendary actor in the heart of the Belgian *pays noir*. It was in Charleroi, the city named after a bewitched, dull Spanish king, where Soëtendrop lost his footing. And it was there that he made his final exit from the stage, too.

Yosee sent me a long, poignant letter, along with a clipping of the obituary published in *De Telegraaf*, where Soëtendrop's disappearance—in Brussels it made headlines and was dubbed *De verdwijning*—is recorded in detail. I read what he had sent me about the life, and the death, and the deceit, and I put it away. There Yosee's style is succinct, affable, yet also agonizing—a reflection not only of the way his mind works but of the debates we used to have. He believed Belgian Jews never felt fully at home and were even more at risk given the rapidly growing number of Muslim immigrants. For Yosee, the future was suffocating, unstable.

I've reread attentively what Yosee sent me. That he decided, after all these years, to mail these things to me—I've changed addresses seven times since we last saw each other—might show that friendship triumphs over passing disagreements. But it is also proof that the sparring has not ended, that, clandestinely, Yosee remains eager to prove his point. Or has he finally capitulated and accepted mine?

⌒

Yosee and I met for the first time more than two decades ago on a hike in the Sinai Desert—shortly before the Israeli army invaded Lebanon. He worked in a kibbutz near the Sea of Galilee; I was enrolled at Hebrew University. I believe the next time we saw each other was in Tel Aviv, at a play by Ephraim Kishon. After the show we found a cozy café on Dizengoff Street and talked for hours about the challenges of the Jewish Diaspora since Auschwitz. That he was from Charleroi (although his family moved to Brussels when he was twelve) and I from Mexico City allowed for humorous exchanges. Neither of us was fully comfortable in Hebrew, his Spanish was a path filled with puddles, and I could make myself understood in Dutch with the help of a *heymish* Yiddish, but only after a couple of beers. Our common ground was an invented language that sounded like Edmund Wilson translating *Eugene Onegin* back into Russian from Vladimir Nabokov's literal English rendition. Later Yosee and I traveled to Massada, then went for a swim in the Dead Sea. It was during that trip that he mentioned wanting to return to Belgium, selling his belongings, and coming back to Israel to make aliyah. "Only in Israel is the Jew safe from adversity," I remember him saying.

When I left Jerusalem after my first year as a student, Yosee happened to be on the same flight to Munich. We spent the time talking about the works of art the Nazis had stolen from collectors and shipped to Prague, which they hoped to turn into a museum of the "lost Jewish race." We parted, I backpacked around Europe on my own, and some months later I visited him and his family in Brussels, where I stayed in an apartment that belonged to a school pal of his a few blocks from Rue Royale, within walking distance of the Gare du Nord. At some point during my weeklong stay Yosee took me to see a performance of *The Misanthrope* with Soëtendrop in the lead role. My friend told me that Soëtendrop was one of the best actors in Belgium and that he knew him, for the two had met in Jerusalem. Tour guides fluent in Dutch, the neutral tongue of the majority of Belgian visitors, were difficult to find in Israel those days.

Yosee not only spoke the language, but was also passionate about biblical archaeology, so while in the kibbutz he had been hired by an agency to moonlight as a Dutch guide.

Soëtendrop, Yosee said, was a powerful presence in the group, not because of his temperament—he could be at once charming and abrasive—but as a result of his fame. "Everyone has seen the movie *Doktor Travistok!* at least twice," my friend claimed, then categorically stated: "He's outstanding as the absentminded scientist." The Old City was a natural rendezvous that brought people together and it seemed to nurture a relationship between Yosee and Soëtendrop. Back in Brussels, the actor invited my friend to his home in Deventer, where he met Soëtendrop's wife Natalie. That same year they celebrated Hanukkah together and were served a meal Yosee described as a "bacchanal," with latkes the size of a salmon, Spanish cheeses, an asparagus soup, a soufflé, a salad with boysenberries. Soëtendrop's portions, Yosee believed, were nothing short of gargantuan. "Jews and food—eternal companions. At one point Maarten looked like a Rembrandt creation." As it turns out, it was the last time my friend saw the actor in person.

As Molière's Alceste, I found Soëtendrop extravagant. He played the role on mannerisms. His corpulence was stressed through hirsute clothes, before engaging in a dialogue he oscillated the neck like a hyena devouring her prey, and he improvised a slight stutter around the letter *t*. Maybe because my friend had recounted their adventures in Jerusalem, I imagined him to be loud, even obnoxious, offstage. "As I get to know him better, he appears to me to be uncomfortable with himself in *real life*, as if body and soul refused to match." Yosee underscored the two words as if for Maarten Soëtendrop the border between this world and the imaginary one had already been blurred. I remember thinking: Do all actors suffer from a similar sense of unreality? In any case, the fact that my friend knew Soëtendrop in person made Molière palatable. After the performance, Yosee asked me if I was ready to greet the actor in his dressing room. I declined, for unless I'm paid to represent them, I never quite know what to say to celebrities.

It seems that Soëtendrop's vanishing act was methodically planned over several weeks. His obesity doesn't appear to have been an obstacle, for his movements were agile, even when at the hospital after his ordeal. He was a master of make-believe. Did he ever doubt his talent to conjure a parallel truth, to make people think he, the most revered of thespians in Belgium, had been mistreated by a horde of hooligans? Only if one were convinced that he knew the distinction between truth and lies. "It is Maarten's sense of morality that is in need of urgent reevaluation," Yosee believes.

The basic facts are uncontestable. On the frigid Thursday evening of December 3, 1987, the police commissioner of

the industrial city of Charleroi announced in a hastily or-
chestrated press conference that Soëtendrop, on tour as Sir
John Falstaff in *The Merry Wives of Windsor*, had not arrived at his usual 6:30 P.M. call before that evening's performance. Thirty-five minutes later, the floor manager
alerted the theater producer who, aware of the actor's
tempestuous personality—yet conscious of his unrivaled
punctuality—called for patience. The hotel where the actor was staying was put on alert. Repeated calls were made
to his room and, eventually, with the producer's permis-
sion, the room was searched. Furthermore, a bar and a
restaurant Soëtendrop frequented were also contacted. At
8:15 P.M. the evening performance was canceled and, soon
after, a search was announced. Since the police commissioner didn't want the media to find out avant la lettre, he
himself let the word out: "Maarten Soëtendrop is a distinguished star. It is too early in the investigation to draw
conclusions. We're hoping for the actor's safe and speedy
return." A freelance reporter dismissed the police commissioner's search as premature. "When a Muslim goes missing near a mine in Bois du Cazier, do the police bother?"
Any misgivings were swiftly put to rest the following
morning the minute the mailman delivered an envelope
to the office of Rabbi Awraham Frydman, some fifty-five
miles north of the city. A carelessly typed note containing
a single line claimed Maarten Soëtendrop was held by the
Flemish Fascist Youth Front.

News of the disappearance touched a nerve in Belgium. The Saturday newspapers offered profiles of the actor's life and career, reflected on the ideology of the previously unknown neo-Nazi group, pondered its whereabouts, and speculated about the chances of its assassinating the famous Flemish actor. In the following days a series of equally muddled notes arrived at the homes of other Jewish leaders, a TV anchor, some members of the Chamber of Representatives, and at Natalie Soëtendrop's. (In one note a quote in French from the Belgian constitution [section 2, article 15] was added: *Nul ne peut être contraint de concourir d'une manière quelconque aux actes et aux cérémonies d'un culte, ni d'en observer les jours de repos.*) After she received the note, Natalie begged the kidnappers for mercy. She urged the Belgian government to act immediately yet responsibly.

"During World War II, Belgium engaged in a silence that turned us into accomplices," Yosee writes in his letter. "This time around, people were eager to shout."

In a display of solidarity, a demonstration took place in the Netherlands, at a church in Amsterdam, on Saturday, December 12—more than a week after Soëtendrop's exit in Charleroi. It attracted politicians and celebrities. The Speaker of the Belgian Parliament described the fascist group as "rats coming out of a hole." Soon after, the justice minister spoke about appointing a special prosecutor to investigate neo-Nazi activities.

With a voracious appetite for beef, Chilean wine, and attention, Maarten Soëtendrop had turned fifty-two on the day of his last performance in Charleroi as Falstaff. In three more days he was scheduled to travel along with the theater company to the cities of Liège, Antwerp, and Ghent. As an actor, he had an esteemed reputation as much for his thespian technique—he was a loyalist of "The Method"—as for his choice of roles. Audiences knew him not only for *Doktor Travistok!* but for films like *White Madness, Walpurgis,* and *The Night of the Birds.* There were reports he was under contract to be in *Amsterdamned.* Furthermore, Soëtendrop was the impresario behind *Aunt Julie,* a successful season of a lesser-known Pirandello play, and the musical *Anatevka,* based on Sholem Aleichem's Yiddish novel *Tevye the Dairyman.* His favorite playwright was Chekhov.

The obituary in *De Telegraaf* describes Soëtendrop as the product of "a mixed background": a Jewish father— also an actor—and a Christian mother. "The embodiment of a divided spirit," Yosee states. In 1940, when Soëtendrop was five and his brother Hugo almost three, their mother abandoned the family abruptly. She had been having an affair with a married man for quite some time—a Nazi collaborator called Siegbert Himmelstrup. Soon after, she filed for divorce and married her lover in 1944. The brothers were separated. Hugo stayed in Brussels where he lived with his mother, stepfather, and his three children.

Maarten was sent to a farm near Leeuwarden, in northern Holland, where for almost two years he was hidden from the Germans by a family. According to Yosee, the episode became a source of shame. "In his eyes, Judaism was about secrecy. His was a servant's mentality. He was hidden because he was inferior." After the war, he lived in Antwerp with a paternal uncle for a little over two years. Eventually Soëtendrop was sent to a boarding school in Bordeaux. In the sixties, he sought out his father in order to talk about his half-Jewish self. His infatuation with drama, he trusted, came from being an outsider—a foreigner—in Belgian culture. He needed his father's approval to remain on the edges, to peek in, to be aloof yet have the gravitas needed to impersonate other characters, not only himself. The father welcomed him but chose not to answer Soëten-drop's questions about the past. "Silence . . . Is it right to define it as the absence of sound? Isn't it an existential condition?"

The obituary mentions a rather pallid, unforthcoming autobiographical essay Soëtendrop published in 1991 in an obscure theater journal called *Wertewelt des Judentums*. According to Yosee, in it Soëtendrop mentions that in 1979, already a promising actor on the Brussels theater scene, he underwent a religious conversion on the eve of Yom Kippur. At that time Soëtendrop was still single, for although he had expressed his love to several women, he had never proposed marriage to any of them. Later on he surveyed an existential vacuum inside himself. "I had lost touch with the inner voice," Yosee quotes him. Soëtendrop found out that the Jewish holidays were about to take place. Formally dressed, with tennis shoes appropriate for the occasion, the actor entered a synagogue in the working-class Anderlecht district, which teemed with Muslim immigrants. Never in his life had he been exposed to prayer, and the Kol Nidre melody sweetened his heart. It was a few months later that he visited Jerusalem with Yosee as his guide. A friend gave him a copy of *The Star of Redemption,* by German philosopher Franz Rosenzweig, which he read with difficulty but admiration. He started therapy with a psychoanalyst called Hermann Musaph. Unexpectedly, the sessions ratified his faith.

In 1987, in the early days of winter, Soëtendrop was in a state of stupor. In an interview, Natalie Soëtendrop portrayed him as "taciturn, under duress," yet when pressed by reporters she refused to be more specific. The reticence turned out to be a stroke of luck. His Falstaff was universally applauded by critics all over Belgium and tickets quickly sold out. The same day he disappeared, a lengthy encomium appeared in the magazine *Dag Allemaal.*

What transpired while Soëtendrop was purportedly a hostage of the F.F.Y.F. is still the subject of conjecture and gossip. The Brussels police headquarters pushed the investigation in every geographical direction. The typed notes were painstakingly analyzed. Rumors of links of several political entities to the F.F.Y.F. circulated. Journalists looked into Soëtendrop's past for clues. Leads emerged but led nowhere.

Natalie Soëtendrop announced on TV her willingness to pay ransom, no matter the amount. It was rumored that an undisclosed sum made available by the government would be given to the captors to secure the actor's safe return. The justice minister quickly issued a disclaimer: "Belgium doesn't fall prey to ruffians. If the Soëtendrop family is willing to pay, it is free to act as it wishes." Soon after, another typed note arrived at Rabbi Frydman's address. It claimed the kidnappers weren't interested in ransom. Theirs was an ideological struggle "to cleanse the country of rubbish."

Then, on Wednesday, December 21, behind a curtain of snow flurries, a shivering, disheveled, ostensibly bruised Maarten Soëtendrop, noticeably thinner, his hands tied behind his back, feces on his hair, blood on his face, abdomen, and sweater, was discovered by a passerby on a dead-end street near the Groeninge Exhibition Center in the city of Bruges. "I was abducted by hatred," he was quoted as saying.

The reporter for *De Telegraaf,* called Erik Eddelbuettel (who authored the obituary Yosee sent along), was the first on the scene. He was followed by the police, an ambulance, and the forensic squad. It was Eddelbuettel who found a typed note stuck to Soëtendrop's sweater. It appeared to be in Spanish: *Judeos de mierda. ¡Furia!*

"Do you recall the day?" Yosee wonders. "The news was wired all around the globe, including the United States. You sent me a comment on a piece you read in the *New York Times.*"

I was indeed shocked when I read the piece. The memories of the prominent Flemish actor on stage in Brussels came back to me like a comet. His safe return pleased me and I was angry at the publicity the neo-Nazis were receiving at Soëtendrop's expense. I saved the clipping thinking it substantiated my friend Yosee Strigler's belief that, after the creation of the state of Israel, life in the Diaspora was no longer justifiable. I was curious as to Soëtendrop's whereabouts during his absence. What type of torture had he been subjected to? Would he be able to overcome the prolonged periods of depression associated with incidents of this nature?

Needless to say, I couldn't have envisioned the twisted knots behind the affair. A day after his reemergence, Soëtendrop, in better shape but still in the hospital, described being seized at a bar by a single man "about my size, perhaps a bit shorter, and certainly slimmer." He was pushed into a car where he was bound and blindfolded. They ripped off the Star of David he wore around his neck. Later he found himself in a sewer tunnel, daubed with feces, and with a swastika dyed on his chest. He remembered being hit in the stomach, losing consciousness. The humiliation reached a climax when, aware of his surroundings, he was asked to kiss a small photograph of Adolf Hitler.

Natalie Soëtendrop rushed to her husband's side. Actors, politicians, and religious leaders paraded through the hospital. Hermann Musaph was interviewed on TV. "Musaph is a Treblinka survivor," Yosee states. "He told viewers that, with the exception of Poland, more Jews were killed during World War II in Belgium and Holland than anywhere else."

Yosee sent Soëtendrop a greeting card the next day. He never got a response. He later found out the actor received close to three thousand cards just on his first day at the hospital.

⌒

On January 6, a month and three days after Soëtendrop's ordeal began, the actor confessed to his own kidnapping. At two hundred thirty-five pounds, he was extraordinarily elastic. He had come up with the whole thing, from his own injuries to the neo-Nazi commando and the typed notes, including the one in flawed Spanish. Collective sympathy soon became unimpeded animosity. The public was furious; it had trusted its actor, but the play itself turned out to be a lie. New demonstrations plastered the streets. There was talk of retribution. The police department sent Soëtendrop a bill. (It was dutifully paid.) There were swastikas painted at bus stops, and a cemetery was desecrated. In Brussels, the synagogue in the Anderlecht district where Soëtendrop had found his faith during a Yom Kippur service was set on fire by a Molotov cocktail. "Is it a surprise that the actor and his wife failed to respond, retreating to their Deventer residence?" Yosee wonders. "Maarten was ashamed of his deeds but he never found the right words to articulate his emotions. It isn't surprising. When it comes to guilt, are Belgians—even Belgian Jews—capable of those words?"

To describe the rationale behind Maarten Soëtendrop's misguided self-flagellation is to ratify—if proof were needed—that reality invariably outdoes the most baroque of dramaturges. My alibi is that nothing in this story is invented. Eddelbuettel, in the obituary, argues that the actor had been involved in a series of Jewish efforts to block an anti-Semitic play by Rainer Werner Fassbinder, *Garbage, the City and Death,* its debut scheduled in Brussels for 1986. It is about a prostitute, Roma, whose fortunes turn around after her encounter with a Frankfurt speculator for the municipal government called the Rich Jew. Frank, a pimp and Roma's husband, leaves her. Roma then asks her lover to kill her. As a result of his connections, the Rich Jew isn't accused of the crime; instead, Frank is. The play was originally written in 1975. Its anti-Semitism forced officials to block it in Germany. A hurricane of op-ed pieces, letters to the editor, and radio broadcasts decried the blockage as a "suspension of freedom of speech in Belgium." Political pundits talked of the tentacles of a Jewish lobby controlling the government. It was printed by the *Frankfurter Allgemeine Zeitung*. Suhrkamp Press released it in book form. The publisher withdrew it and would not release it until Fassbinder changed the name of the Rich Jew. The director steadfastly refused. In 1984, a couple of years after Fassbinder's death, the Old Opera in Frankfurt attempted to stage it once more. It was again stopped. (In the interim, the Yoram Loewenberg acting school in Israel performed it.) Another company tried to stage it in Belgium soon after without success. An anti-Fassbinder protest led by Rabbi Frydman and supported by Maarten Soëtendrop took hold. There was more censorship. A publisher in Antwerp released it in Dutch translation. In mid-1987 it was read on Belgian public radio. Still, no theater agreed to produce Fassbinder's play.

"What are the uses of hatred?" Yosee asks in his letter. "Maarten's intentions were good. His ploy might have forced a referendum in the Netherlands, the land of Baruch Spinoza and Anne Frank, but not in Belgium, where 'the mendacious amnesia'—the phrase was used by Soëtendrop—accumulated over decades remains unexposed. Instead, he ended up being confronted by a tribunal of his own device, one staged in a theater as big as the entire world. He wanted to understand the power of silence. But in this area, he was short of talent."

At the time of the confession, Soëtendrop's lawyer, Luuk Hammer, described his client as being "in a state of panic." But he wasted no time in exculpating him: "Is our illustrious theater star guiltier than the rest of us are? Maarten Soëtendrop may have lost sight of his boundaries. He is an expert in theater but not an expert in crime."

The actor's sole response came after the justice minister requested an "official" apology. Soëtendrop went on camera with an epigrammatic—and, in Yosee's eyes, suspicious—statement on Thursday, May 10, 1988. "If in any way I've offended the Belgian people in particular, and the Low Countries in general, I deeply regret it. My life has been a pandemonium since I was five."

In the obituary in *De Telegraaf,* Eddelbuettel claims Soëtendrop was in the Charleroi sewer system for only three days. Disguised in a woman's clothes (wig, lavender dress, heavy winter coat), he stayed in a homeless shelter until after Christmas Day, then moved to a place on Rue Émile Vandervelde until January 2. Surreptitiously, he broke into his dressing room at the theater at midnight the next day, took makeup equipment, a curtain rope, a knife, and some paint. A night guard reported hearing odd noises but didn't spot him. Fewer than forty-eight hours later, he was already in his thespian apparel in Bruges.

Did Soëtendrop truly repent? Not in Yosee's eyes. "Even when he apologized to the justice minister, I'm convinced Maarten was still acting. In fact, he acted all the way to the grave."

In his letter, my friend offers convincing evidence. It is an indictment of journalistic practices. "Reporters only scratch the surface. They are impatient. Their next deadline is a distraction. Had they bothered to look up the actor's past meticulously," he writes, "they would have come across unsettling data. Did he really devise his own disappearance? He was an intelligent man. But he was haunted. Becoming an actor was a way to alleviate his inner doubts. It allowed him an opportunity to take a regular vacation from himself."

Yosee listed valuable information about Soëtendrop's father, mother, and brother. After a career on the regional stage, his father retired in the seventies and died of an aneurism in 1981. He and his eldest son seldom spoke to each other. The link between Soëtendrop and his mother was even more tenuous. Ostensibly, she, along with one of her grandchildren, visited him after a performance of *Platonov* in Louvain and tried to reintroduce herself. Believing she was a stalker, Soëtendrop avoided her. His mother subsequently attempted another reunion. Although by then the actor knew well who she was, he refused to see her. She died in 1994 while on a trip to Greece.

"The bond with Hugo Soëtendrop is more convoluted," Yosee adds. In *Wertewelt des Judentums*, the sections dedicated to him are called "Pandemonium." They are surveys of their tense relationship, describing Hugo as "a loving brother who learned to loathe." But they conceal more than they reveal. For instance, Soëtendrop stressed—a total of nineteen times—that since he left for the farm near Leeuwarden, he and Hugo never saw each other again. "Why overemphasize the point?"

After Yosee read the autobiographical essay, he sent Soëtendrop a congratulatory note. In it he asked him about his brother. Again, Soëtendrop failed to respond. Yosee was intrigued, though. He looked for the name Hugo Soëtendrop in the national birth registry; he found it. Then he searched telephone records; this time he came up empty-handed. A reference in a school yearbook in Kortrijk led him to one François Soëten; it was a dead end. Another one in Roeselare talked about a Sutendorp brewing company. He then searched for Soëtendrop's stepfather, Siegbert Himmelstrup. An entire dossier became available. He identified Himmelstrup as a metal worker in Antwerp, a sixty-seven-year-old devout Catholic, married with four children: Heinrich, Julian, Ute, and Elfriede. A series of archived photographs gave Yosee the certitude he wanted: Hugo Soëtendrop had been baptized—and reeducated—

as Julian Himmelstrup and had been a member of the Nazi Youth League. After the war he studied engineering in Bielefeld, Westphalia, and eventually returned to Brussels. For a short while in the eighties he lived in Madrid, where he signed up for a four-week course on the Spanish Civil War. "I was rewarded with a nemesis," Yosee writes. "Hugo lived in Bruges, where he was a part-time employee at the Federal Department of the Environment. He was divorced by then and I know little about his first wife. He tried to have a child with a second wife, but it took its toll and after three miscarriages she left him. Estranged from everyone, Hugo lived in a rented room near Rue Émile Vandervelde. Like his stepfather, whom he adored, his support for Nazism didn't diminish after the war. Indeed, until the end he believed Hitler's overall mission to racially improve Europe would one day be accomplished in toto."

Hugo followed his brother's career with a mix of wonder and resentment. He kept a distance because Soëtendrop's renewed faith in Judaism disgusted him. His reluctance to get involved changed in the aftermath of the anti-Fassbinder protests. In Hugo's view, Belgium made an irreversible pact with the devil when *Garbage, the City and Death* was canceled.

Knowing Soëtendrop was scheduled to be part of a rally organized by Rabbi Frydman, Hugo hid amid the crowd. Did Soëtendrop spot him, too? Hugo heard his brother give a speech about the perils of amnesia. "It was then that he plotted Maarten's kidnapping," Yosee writes. "Or is it the other way around? I confess to be on shaky ground in this area of my search. But that doesn't make it less believable. I've discovered, for instance, that Hugo— aka Julian Himmelstrup—gave final notice to the Federal Department of the Environment on December 27, 1987. The room he rented was vacated the day before. 'An old woman took everything with her,' the owner told me. 'She said Monsieur Himmelstrup was indisposed. As long as she gave me the last monthly pay, I didn't care to ask for specifics.' The Olivetti used for typing the notes pur- portedly written by the Flemish Fascist Youth Front was found."

That cold afternoon in Charleroi on December 3, Hugo caught up with his sibling, his tipsy older—and odder—self, at a bar on the way to the theater. "Did Maarten recognize him? There is no way to know. Julian Himmelstrup was, unlike his brother, thin, pale, and with teeth even the British would abhor. He was a nobody. That afternoon he was wearing a fedora. Probably neither of them thought the encounter would last long. I've tried to imagine the dialogue they engaged in, but it isn't easy in a generation taught not to use words. They walked a few blocks together and then they disappeared. I don't think *De verdwijning* was a fait accompli in the mind of either of them, as the media led us to believe. Things were impro- vised, the way they often are when madness sets in. But this kind of madness was more coherent, more intelligible. One of them—was it Maarten?—let his pathos run wild. Ah, the media! Is there a less trustworthy theater? Are we all fooled more often by any other device? I don't trust the interviews granted by Natalie Soëtendrop, Luuk Hammer, anyone . . . To me it looks as if they, I, and everyone had been fortuitously invited to a performance in the biggest theater imaginable. Harry Mulisch, who won the Prijs van de Nederlandse Letteren in 1995, published a novella-cum-play (he calls it 'a contradiction') made of a pair of monologues and an intermezzo. It is narrated at Soëtendrop's funeral. Maarten becomes Herbert Althans and Natalie becomes Magda. But it distorts the intricacy of events This is because literature is always a game. Why distort what has already been misrepresented?"

Yosee bluntly visualizes the scene in which the siblings have reached the Charleroi sewer system. "The city was built in 1666, the year in which the pseudomessiah Sabbatai Zevi—who eventually became an apostate by converting to Islam—expected the world to come to an end. At the time Spain ruled the Low Countries. The idea was to build a fortification in order to stop the imperial troops of Louis XIV. The sewer system is a macabre web made of symmetrical dungeons. Maarten and Hugo walked the maze until they found a large, dank chamber where the air was fetid. There was only a sliver of light. The memory of the Hanukkah 'bacchanal' I spent with Maarten and

Natalie lies in sharp contrast in my mind. For hours they stared at each other's shadows. Had they done anything else in life? Then Maarten probably said: 'I thought I killed you inside me a long time ago. But when I saw your face in the crowd, I realized I was wrong. After we expiate the guilt we've been forced to inherit—what the Germans call *Schuld*—only one of us is likely to emerge from this darkness.'"

The final paragraph of Yosee's letter is the most eloquent. "So there you have it: another retelling of Cain and Abel. Before his death in a hotel in Charleroi, on Rue de la Providence, Maarten was dangerously overweight—close to three hundred pounds, according to Eddelbuettel. In the last few years the public recognized him mostly for his soap endorsements on TV. And I know little else except that on the High Holidays he and Natalie prayed at Brussels's elegant Sephardic synagogue on Rue du Pavillon and that he donated money to the Belgian Jewish Museum to buy back art stolen by the Nazis. And, of course, Maarten remained an assiduous patron of the most refined French restaurants. Did he sin through the mouth to compensate for the lack of words? These questions have no answer. When did Maarten come up with the F.F.Y.F.? Who typed the notes sent to his wife, Rabbi Frydman, and others? It doesn't matter. The fact is Hugo was never seen again. I've checked hospices, morgues, crime logs. He seems to have vanished into smoke. In our debates, Ilan, I always took the stand that Israel would finally solve the dilemmas of the Diaspora. It would make the Jew beautiful, a bronze man, a warrior. Our ancient sense of inferiority—the metaphorical hunchback we've carried with us for generations and generations—would be disposed once and for all: no more apologies, no more inferiority complexes. As you know, I tried to live up to my opinions by making aliyah. It didn't work. I became a lawyer who specializes in Holocaust reparation cases. I wanted to do some good after the pervasiveness of evil. But evil is an essential component of Nature, the opposite of good. One can't exist without the other. All things considered, I'm a diasporic creature like you, one comfortable looking at things as an outsider. For centuries Jews kept the prohibition against idolatry. Among other things, this meant that acting was forbidden. To be someone else, even for a short while, is to compete with the Almighty's creation. The prohibition backfired; at heart, all Jews are actors. The art of impostures is encoded in our DNA. How else could we exist with the contradictions that inhabit us? In what other way would we pretend to live a happy life among strangers and still dwell in our unique unhappiness? Maarten's odyssey frightens me. He put on a serious face in front of millions while pretending to have been kidnapped. People believed him. But who ended up losing?"

Yosee Strigler's letter was postmarked in Israel.

The answer is always a form of death.

   John Fowles, *The Magus*, 1965

morirse está en hebreo

FOR ABRAHAM SLOMIANSKI, זײַל

The Funeral

Death caught up with Moishe Tartakovsky, a wealthy leather businessman and the proud owner of a well-rounded belly the size of a *sandía*, less than a month after his seventieth birthday.

It was Friday, around 9:30 A.M. Moishe was at the Centro Deportivo Israelita, best known by its initials, C.D.I., the Jewish sports center in Mexico City where Moishe spent his mornings swimming laps and walking on the track, and the afternoons playing poker.

The shriek that followed his sudden collapse, a frightful, desperate *"¡Dios mío, un muerto!"* was uttered by an anonymous passerby, an athlete with brand-new, flashy Nike sneakers. The sound didn't reach Elías Fischer, the owner of a restaurant chain, Moishe's childhood friend and accountant, and a man who people always said looked like Jimmy Stewart, until several seconds later. It took a few more instants for Fischer to make the connection. *"Ay, ¿y si el caído fuera mi cuate?"*

The night before the two had dined together at an elegant restaurant near Moishe's apartment in the Polanco neighborhood. He laughed and joked until the late hours. When Fischer saw him again on the track, he looked like a bull. "I'm ready to seize the day," Moishe said before each started his exercise routine. They would greet each other every time they crossed paths on the track, and by 10:15 A.M., they would be ready to take a shower.

Once it dawned on him that Moishe might have had a heart attack, Fischer ran full speed. He begged: "You shouldn't die. What will your family do without you?" He tried pumping Moishe's chest, giving him mouth-to-mouth resuscitation. It was useless. Holding his friend's head in his lap, a sentence Fischer once heard crossed his mind: *Dios propone y el hombre dispone.* Randomly, he wondered if Moishe's death had been the result of God's hiccup. The idea came to him because in the previous Yom Kippur sermon, Rabbi Sapotnik, the Buenos Aires–trained leader of Congregación Beit Yitzhak, described the insignificance of human life in those terms: "The Almighty shakes and his creatures are shaken," the rabbi said.

In spite of the traffic on a hectic Friday morning, the Red Cross ambulance with two paramedics took fewer than ten minutes to arrive. "What an asshole!" Fischer thought. "You can't call an ambulance. They'll want to take the body with them." It had been the guard at the main entrance who, through a walkie-talkie, asked a colleague to dial 066. Everyone knew already that the victim had died. The body needed to be taken to the morgue, not to a hospital. Even though the guard had been working at C.D.I. for three months, nobody had cared to tell him that Jews cannot end up in the morgue.

Fischer was standing by. "There's nothing to do, señor," the paramedic in charge announced. The second paramedic was assessing the damage while gathering the necessary information on the appropriate medical forms. "The Servicio Médico Forense has been alerted," the one in charge said. "They should be here any minute. It is its responsibility to take him away and perform the autopsy."

"There won't be any autopsy, I'm sorry to say," Fischer responded. "I'll take care of him. The Jewish faith forbids tinkering with a body."

The two paramedics made a gesture of impatience. One of them stated: "The deceased is in the State of Mexico. The law is the law. He must be under the jurisdiction of the forensic unit."

"I doubt it," Fischer replied. "My dear friend Moishe Tartakovsky, may his soul rest in peace, lived as a Jew and died as a Jew. His body is under *my* jurisdiction. Plus, the Centro Deportivo Israelita is right on the border of Distrito Federal and the State of Mexico. Do you want me to prove it to you in the *Guía Roji*?"

The Red Cross crew was visibly frustrated. "Everybody in Mexico is Christ's child," the second assistant announced, raising his voice.

"Believe me, this one is not," Fischer stated in an even louder tone.

Hugo Bergman, the C.D.I. treasurer and Moishe's poker buddy, joined in the conversation. He happened to have finished getting a massage and pedicure when he heard rumors that the body on the track belonged to none other than Moishe Tartakovsky.

"I'm a doctor," Bergman lied. "I work at the Hospital Inglés." He proceeded to inspect the body. "Don't worry! This man is my patient. He suffers from seizures. He's alive!"

The statement shocked the paramedics. When they asked him for his medical ID, Bergman said it was in the locker room.

Distracted at first, Fischer didn't catch his meaning until a few seconds had gone by. "Moishe is alive?" he asked.

Bergman winked. "Yes . . . Please leave it up to me!"

But it was already too late again. In the hoopla, the two paramedics placed the body inside the ambulance and it was gone in no time at all.

Fischer remembered hearing from the paramedic in charge that the body would be stored in a refrigerator until the autopsy was completed.

"*¡Puta madre!*" Bergman said. "For him to get a proper burial, a monstrous bureaucracy will need to be fought."

By afternoon, the Tartakovsky family was coping with the inevitable—rescuing Moishe from the morgue while making the necessary preparations for the *levaya*. It took exactly sixteen hours and twenty-three minutes for the former to be accomplished. The latter was faster and easier; Fischer called Rabbi Sapotnik, who in turn let the Chevrah Kadishah handle all the logistics. Fortunately, the Sabbath stood between Moishe's death and his descent to his final resting place. The funeral was thus scheduled for Sunday.

Mexico was in turmoil. A heated presidential election, one with dramatic implications, was about to take place. People everywhere were excited by the radical transformation about to happen in a country known for its electoral apathy. Ernesto Zedillo, the incumbent president, had finally refused to engage in *el dedazo,* and the P.R.I., the ruling party, handpicked his successor. The break with tradition gave other parties a power they never imagined, in particular the P.A.N., the center-right party. Vicente Fox, its candidate, was a former Coca-Cola executive with little experience in politics.

On Saturday, Rosita Shein, Moishe's high school sweetheart, who over the years had tried to hide her wrinkles by flying to San José, Costa Rica, to have *el embellecimiento,* as she called it—an embellishment with a world-renowned specialist, the son of a legendary TV actress, and who was famous for operating on his own mother's face a total of seventeen times—parked her Porsche a couple of blocks away from Moishe's apartment. They had dated for three months when she was seventeen, but years ago she ceased being in love with him. He would be the perfect husband for her, even though her parents thought she could find someone who wasn't an immigrant, someone with a more secure financial background. She refused to listen to them. However, hell broke loose when she revealed to him that she had been intimate with her previous boyfriend and was no longer a virgin. Moishe was shocked and they broke up a couple of days later.

Even though she ended up marrying an optician—who, as it turned out, was a philanderer whom she divorced before her oldest child was Bar Mitzvah—Rosita made Moishe a promise before their relationship collapsed: If you die first, I'll make sure you're laid to rest in peace. It was a premonition. By the time Moishe died, he had been a widower for twelve years. Also, in the last few months of his life, and maybe even for as long as a year, he had ceased contact with his rambunctious son Bernardo (called affectionately in Yiddish "Berele"), and with his daughter Esther and her husband Enrique he talked only occasionally. His encounters with his grandchildren were no less infrequent.

Rosita rang the bell. Trinidad, Moishe's attractive twenty-five-year-old maid, who as usual was wearing her white-and-blue uniform with a padded apron on top, buzzed her in. She rode the elevator to the penthouse.

"Trini, *chula*. Don Moishe is dead. For seven days scores of people will mourn him in this apartment."

"Will it be with an open casket?" Trini asked.

"Among the Jews the burial takes place immediately. Once it finishes, the family will spend the week together."

"Muy bien, señora."

"You knew don Moishe died, didn't you?" Rosita asked.

"Yes, don Bernardo called me. It's sad . . ."

"At what time did he wake up on Friday?"

"Don Moishe?"

"Yes," Rosita responded.

"He didn't sleep in the apartment that night."

"He didn't?"

"No . . . He often slept somewhere else."

"Where?"

"I didn't ask."

"With señora Mabel?"

"I don't know."

Rosita was puzzled but didn't want to appear indiscreet. She and the maid spent the afternoon moving furniture. Esther Burak, Moishe's daughter, a well-rounded forty-eight-year-old woman of gentle manners who walked pigeon-toed, arrived at 4:30 P.M. After commiserating over tea and cookies with Rosita, she covered the mirrors with blankets, put the sofa pillows on the floor, and brought out stools and folding chairs.

Sunday began unusually humid. People started gathering in the Jewish cemetery on Avenida Constituyentes shortly after 11:00 A.M. The solemnity, of course, was unavoidable. The family gathered in the room where the members of the Chevrah Kadishah were washing Moishe's body.

"He looks thinner than when I last saw him," Enrique, Moishe's son-in-law, a respected ophthalmologist in his early fifties, said to his wife.

"When did we see him last?" Esther asked.

"Maybe three months ago?"

At that moment, Fischer was standing outside. *"¡Ich bin doh!"* he uttered in Yiddish. He was wearing a modern suit and black yarmulke. Ari Burak, Esther's oldest son, a pediatrician, overheard him. He and his wife Lorena were talking about Lucy, their six-month-old baby daughter.

"The sheer sight makes me nauseous," Ari told Fischer. "I'm guilty because I know I should be inside."

"Coming from you, Ari, I'm surprised," Fischer responded. "You're a doctor, like your father. If you're incapable of looking at a dead person, what should your patients expect from you?"

Ari and Lorena laughed. "Ironic, isn't it?" he replied. "When I'm in the operating room, I have no problems. Since the patient I'm taking care of isn't connected to me, I do my job without emotion. It only happens with someone I know. When a dear schoolmate, Marcos Reznik, died unexpectedly of an aortic aneurism more than a decade ago, I already had my private practice. I visited him in the hospital numerous times. Once he passed away, though, I couldn't concentrate. For days the image of Marcos imprisoned in the casket obsessed me."

Fischer reacted. "Imprisoned?"

"I would dream of Marcos's lungs. What if they suddenly started to inflate again?"

"Death makes us come to a standstill."

"Except for the memory of those left behind. It is only natural that they would refuse to give up an image known for its incessant movement. Don't we remember the past in motion?"

Ari waited for Fischer's reply but it didn't come. "I heard you say '*¡Ich bin doh!*'" he added. "What did you mean?"

"Only a joke. My friendship with your *zeide* dates back . . . *ay,* to our years as students at the Yiddishe Shule. We were classmates. The teachers would take attendance at the beginning of the lesson. A few times when I skipped school, as the roster was being read Moishe imitated my voice and pretended I was present. I did the same when he was absent. In the Spanish lesson we would say '*Presente,*' in the Hebrew one '*Aníh poh,*' and in the Yiddish ones '*Ich bin doh.*' We were never caught."

It was a few minutes before noon and hundreds of people were already at the *levaya*. That a political march on Avenida Reforma, in opposition to the P.R.I.'s presidential candidate—planned several days in advance and announced on TV and radio stations—was scheduled for that Sunday didn't seem to stop any mourner from attending.

37

"I'm impressed by the quantity," Ari said.

"Why?" Fischer wondered.

"I never thought *Zeide* knew this many people. My impression of him was of a loner. After *Bobe* Hilda died, I visualized him in his apartment."

"Moishe's skin made him look younger than he was. He was a loyal friend . . ."

"I knew he liked to travel."

"In the last few years, he visited Russia, India, China, Brazil . . ." Fischer commented.

"Alone?"

"Mostly."

"How do you travel alone? What do you do with your time?" Ari inquired.

"The same you do with others, I assume," Fischer responded.

People were a bit impatient until Rabbi Sapotnik announced that the *taharah,* the purification the body needed to undergo before the burial, was still not completed. It would be at least twenty minutes before the *levaya* would get started.

Ari took a deep breath and entered the room where the members of the Chevrah Kadishah were performing the ritual. A bucket of water and several memorial candles were placed near the body. He heard someone ask Berele, Moishe's oldest child and the heir to his leather factory, for his father's *talit.*

"I apologize, but I don't know if he had one."

"All Jewish men ought to have one."

"Moishe wasn't religious."

"So?"

"He believed in culture," Berele answered.

"Tradition says that the deceased should be wrapped in his prayer shawl."

"Why not use a ranchero *sarape*?" Berele asked.

A silence ensued. Berele realized his comment was sacrilegious. "Will my own *talit* do?"

"Your *talit* is reserved for your own departure. An old one from the cemetery will need to be used."

Moishe's nails were cut, his hair combed. His body was washed and then wrapped in a white-and-blue shroud, its fringes trimmed to indicate that the deceased was no longer bound by any religious obligation. A small bag of soil from Israel was placed in a rough, unassuming coffin, and Rabbi Sapotnik read a prayer: *"Hamakon Yenajen, Betoj Shaar Aele Tzion Virushalain."*

The casket was raised by the members of the Chevrah Kadishah while one of them poured twenty-four quarts of water from a bucket over it. After this, the congregants recited three times:

"Tahor hoo."

Someone added in Yiddish: "We are hereby the last ones to see Moishe . . . Like Moishe Rabeynu, after whom he was named, he is finally free, in this Mount Sinai, beyond all forms of human chaos, and thus until the arrival of the Messiah."

Ari had studied Moishe's facial expression. Was there sarcasm in it? Esther, his mother, was nearby. "Was *Zeide* smiling?"

Before she was able to answer, Rabbi Sapotnik said: "*Nireh v'eyno ro'he.*' The dead have an enviable quality—they are seen but cannot see."

As the coffin was carried out of the room, and, as they were heading in the direction of the grave, mourners could hear the marchers on the street shouting slogans: "*¡Abajo el P.R.I.! ¡Bienvenido el cambio!*"

Once near the final resting place, Berele positioned himself next to Esther, who was hiding the pain behind her sunglasses. "Do you think *La Goye* will come?" he asked.

"Will you call her by her name? She's human, like you and me. I'm not so sure about you, Berele," Esther replied. "You started it all. After Mother died, he followed your path . . ."

"Good for him," he said. "There isn't much of an option, *hermana.* Mexican Jewish women are a bore!"

"Berele, are you sure you're able to cope with Moishe's death?"

"I'm perfectly fine," he responded in an aggressive tone. "Thanks for asking. How about you?"

An athletic fifty-one-year-old with a virile physique, his hair rapidly receding, Berele was famous for his troubled relationship with Moishe. Nothing Berele did ever satisfied his father. In Moishe's eyes he wasn't bright enough, assertive enough, dependable enough, self-motivated enough. Actually, Moishe felt pity for his son. His experience as an immigrant forced him to seize upon every opportunity. Berele, instead, was a *vividor*. After taking over his father's business, he squandered the capital. Eventually, the factory burned to the ground. For years rumors circulated that it had been arson but Berele managed to collect the insurance money anyway.

Rabbi Sapotnik again approached Berele. "I need you, Bernardo. Moishe's soul requires your attention. Jews have a share in the World to Come," he said, "as it is stated in the *Book of Isaiah:* Thy people are righteous, they shall inherit the Earth forever.'"

"Is anyone exempted?" Berele asked.

"Only those who deny the resurrection of the dead."

"I don't want Moishe to resurrect," he argued. "He's done enough damage."

Esther overheard him. "Berele, behave yourself."

Berele added: "Once on this Earth is more than enough."

A few miles away, the Volkswagen was already on its way to the funeral. Enrique's chauffeur had picked up Nicolás and Galia at the airport. He was a twenty-eight-year-old Orthodox Jew from Jerusalem, tall and nervous-looking, with big ears like Dumbo; she a twenty-six-year-old, natural blonde, slim, medium-sized film student from New York. They hadn't seen each other since Nicolás abruptly left Mexico in 1989. Needless to say, Galia was shocked by his looks, as she remembered him as an average *paisano,* dressed in typical jeans, sneakers, and T-shirt, a music fan who collected LPs of Styx and Earth, Wind and Fire. "What strange bug bit my *primo*?" she wondered. In Upper Manhattan, where she lived in a one-bedroom apartment a few blocks from Columbia University, she crossed paths with dozens of Orthodox Jews, although probably not as many as those pullulating around 47th Street. In fact, every so often she talked to one of them, a proselytizer from the Mitzvah Mobile parked on Broadway and 116th Street. He wanted her to attend synagogue on the Sabbath. Were there any Orthodox Jews in Mexico in the eighties, in the La Herradura subdivision, when she was growing up? Not that she remembered. In any case, she couldn't have imagined her estranged cousin becoming a religious fanatic, dressed in black, with *peyes* and a long beard.

For a few minutes a traffic light on Avenida Reforma brought the Volkswagen to a standstill. A vendor selling crucifixes approached the chauffeur. Nicolás looked elsewhere to evade the image.

"He couldn't have known you're Jewish. Or could he?"

"Welcome back to Mexico, *primo,*" Galia said. "Security is tighter than when you were last here, more than a decade ago." Nicolás looked at her with displeasure.

Realizing his customers weren't interested in his mer-

chandise, the vendor brought out a Star of David neck-
lace. Nicolás looked at it carefully, then rejected it. Galia
laughed out loud: "To think that there are around thirty-
five thousand Mexican Jews like you and me nationwide.
Un número minúsculo. Not even one percent of the overall
population."

"It isn't the numbers that count," Nicolás responded.
"Faith matters in the eyes of the Almighty even if only just
one believer is alive on Earth."

"You must be right," she replied. "The vendor is astute
enough to find his small but wealthy clientele."

She proceeded to buy the Star of David. "A souvenir
for you, Nicolasito. In the Mexico of today, religion is for
sale."

As the chauffeur speeded along back ways, the Volkswagen stumbled upon thousands of demonstrators, now
not only denouncing the P.R.I. but American imperialism
as well. *"¡Viva la soberanía nacional!"* Finally, it parked outside the cemetery. Nicolás and Galia hurried in.

Busy on a cellular conversation, Berele made a sign to
Enrique who spotted the cousins and notified Rabbi Sapotnik. "Everything is in place," he said.

"Okay, it is time to perform the *k'riah* and pray."

The rabbi requested the Tartakovsky clan to rip the
fabric of their clothes while singing Dayan ha-Emet. He
then walked toward Berele, who was leaning on a large
nondescript tombstone. The rabbi asked him to stop using

the cell phone and to come closer because, whether he liked it or not, he was responsible for reciting the Kaddish.

The rabbi commented: "I believe your father died without a Vidduy, a deathbed confession. As you might know, among Jews there is no requirement for a final rite. If the dying person isn't able to recite it, there is no transgression. The soul isn't in jeopardy. However, Moishe's soul, in its journey, might seek ways to communicate his last wishes before it departs from this world. It is crucial that everyone pay attention to any supernatural signal. Moishe might be anxious to talk to us. Throughout the *levaya* and the shivah, the soul will pursue its ascent to Heaven."

"Come on, rabbi!" Berele stated. "This is the twenty-first century."

Rabbi Sapotnik wasn't pleased with Berele's overall behavior. "Will you at least recite the Kaddish? The *Shulhan Aruch* recommends that one recite it when death is imminent. 'God of my Fathers and Mothers, may my prayer come before You. Do not ignore my plea. Please, forgive me for all that I sinned before You throughout my life.' If your father, *alav hashalom*, was unable to say the Vidduy, the Almighty will embrace him. But it is your duty to pray for his soul."

"My son Nicolás will do it!" he announced.

Just then a violinist, stepping out from the crowd, approached the place where Rabbi Sapotnik was standing. He placed the round part of his instrument under his chin,

located with his fingers the appropriate notes, and began
to play. It was a fragment from Ernest Bloch's *Violin Con-
certo in A minor.* The sound of the violin was hypnotizing
and people who had been sharing their thoughts with each
other minutes before were now quiet.

Once the music ended Rabbi Sapotnik spoke. He described what a Jewish funeral was supposed to accom-
plish—peace and unity between this world and the next.
He then recited several prayers. Nicolás had moved forward, leaving Galia behind. He had given his father a lukewarm embrace. Meanwhile, she approached her own parents, Esther and Enrique, and kissed them affectionately.
She was delighted to see them even under these circum
stances.

A few minutes later Nicolás whispered something into
Rabbi Sapotnik's ear. A second later, the rabbi made a gesture of consent.

"I wish to read a poem in Hebrew by Shmuel ha-
Naguid, once the vizier of Granada, who died in 1056,"
Nicolás said. "It's called 'Short Prayer in Time of Battle.'"
He read it in Hebrew and then translated the last line: "If
I am not deserving in Your eyes—do it for the sake of my
son and my sacred learning."

Rabbi Sapotnik picked up on the lines as he looked
deeply into Berele's eyes: "Do it for the sake of my son and
my sacred learning." Then he began his sermon. With
endearing yet cautionary words he portrayed Moishe as a

responsible, beloved Jew and a grateful Mexican, a heroic builder of the community without whose work today's generation of Ashkenazi Jews would not be as comfortable—"perhaps *too* comfortable." He added: "Moishe Tartakovsky wasn't a devout Jew but he was a moral Jew. He was also a patriarch . . ."

Standing near her mother, Galia whispered: "A patriarch? I thought *Zeide* couldn't care less about the Jews . . ."

"Shhhh!" Esther motioned to her daughter.

Rabbi Sapotnik continued: ". . . a patriarch who understood that culture is the conduit through which we perpetuate ourselves in the world. Culture and tradition . . . The exigencies of life hardly ever allow us to seize the full measure of our talents, but he did fine. He was a Lithuanian immigrant who, in 1937 at the age of seven, arrived by steamer in Puerto de Veracruz, in the Gulf of Mexico. Throughout his life, Moishe Tartakovsky displayed zest and intelligence. I'm often asked: Rabbi Sapotnik, is ours an age of miracles? Well, let me tell you about an amazing miracle. Moishe was a peddler who sold shoelaces. With the little money he saved from some batches, he took his biggest risk—he played the lottery and won. He received an award of two hundred pesos, a modest prize, but a prize nonetheless; it was enough to rent space for a shoe shop that eventually became two, three, then a leather factory, and finally a profitable consortium. He started at the end of Plutarco Elías Calles's administration. He leaves us as Mexico is in the middle of a political transformation."

He took a deep breath and continued. "Moishe married Hilda Spigelman in 1951, not three years after the founding of the State of Israel. Hilda gave birth to two children and died in 1988 after a long battle with cancer. The Almighty wants it that he be buried now at her side. Throughout their journey on Earth they not only nurtured a happy family but managed to keep in mind the anguish of others. A magnanimous building in the Eishel, the Jewish Home for the Elderly in Cuernavaca, Morelos, was built thanks to one of Moishe's generous donations, and a large forest in Israel, on the edges of the Negev Desert, sprung to greenness in Hilda's memory with his support. In addition, he donated large amounts to his school, the Yiddishe Shule, as well as to Nicolás's yeshiva in Jerusalem."

Galia was restless once again. "He never sent *me* anything . . . ," she whispered in Esther's ear.

"No one's life is exclusively marked by blissfulness. Like each and every one of us, Moishe underwent periods of distress and despondency. His wife's death left him disoriented, uncommitted, numbed. He asked tough questions, perhaps best exemplified in a quote from the *Talmud* by the first century B.C.E. sage Hillel: 'If I'm not for myself, who will be for me? But if I'm only for myself, who am I?' Like most Jews in Mexico, he went to temple only during the High Holidays, but in the last few months he started to go more regularly, almost every Saturday. He even performed the mitzvah of embracing the *Torah* on a couple of occasions and parading it for the congregation to kiss it. At the end of the service Moishe talked to people about Hillel's emblematic quote. But then, *Reeboynu shel-Oylom,* You took him away from us. There ought to be a reason, of course, for Your actions are never arbitrary, even though they might look to some that way. You allowed Moishe the time and courage to act, and for that we are grateful. That he felt dissatisfied with himself and the world is just a sign of the myriad of possibilities You allow for your creatures. Let us then champion Moishe Tartakovsky as a compassionate Jew, one never fully content with his accomplishments."

Rabbi Sapotnik concluded his sermon with the El Male Rachamim. Berele took a shovel and threw soil on top of the casket. As he passed the shovel along to others, Nicolás recited the first stanza of the Kaddish in his father's stead:

יִתְגַּדַּל וְיִתְקַדַּשׁ שְׁמֵהּ רַבָּא.
בְּעָלְמָא דִּי בְרָא כִרְעוּתֵהּ.
וְיַמְלִיךְ מַלְכוּתֵהּ, בְּחַיֵּיכוֹן וּבְיוֹמֵיכוֹן
וּבְחַיֵּי דְכָל בֵּית יִשְׂרָאֵל,
בַּעֲגָלָא וּבִזְמַן קָרִיב. וְאִמְרוּ אָמֵן:

The mood was somber. The mourners responded to the Kaddish with taciturn voices. Galia let her eyes wander to the tombstones nearby. Several were sprinkled with pebbles.

One included a yellowing photograph in a metal frame of a family of four—a mother and her three boys. There was a fresh bouquet of flowers near the frame and a bee flitting around. The bee projected a nervous shadow on a marble surface. She tried following the shadow but it moved too fast. Suddenly, her mind wandered into a disconnected state in which she considered the existence of the Afterlife. Do we go anywhere after we die? She doubted it. Death for her was an end, not a beginning. Could she be wrong? As of late, she had been reading books on Hinduism. According to the *Bhagavad Gita,* the human soul reincarnates time and again. It might acquire several forms until it becomes perfect. That search for perfection allows it to mutate until it finally embraces the Almighty. A girlfriend she knew in Queens gave her a quote, although Galia didn't remember the exact source: "Just as a man discards worn-out clothes and puts on new clothes, the soul discards worn-out bodies and wears new ones." Did Judaism also believe in reincarnation? She doubted it, although the same girlfriend insinuated that Jewish mystics were closer to Hinduism in their own theology than most of their co-religionists. It might be foolish to believe in reincarnation but at least it placates the suffering a mourner experiences with a beloved's death. If Moishe's soul ever returned to this Earth, would Galia be able to recognize it? Suddenly, she realized the bee had stopped. It was sucking the pollen in a flower's stamen. The thought that the bee and its shadow had become one pleased her. She listened to the Kaddish's last stanza:

יְהֵא שְׁלָמָא רַבָּא מִן שְׁמַיָּא וְחַיִּים
עָלֵינוּ וְעַל כָּל יִשְׂרָאֵל. וְאִמְרוּ אָמֵן:
עֹשֶׂה שָׁלוֹם בִּמְרוֹמָיו הוּא יַעֲשֶׂה שָׁלוֹם
עָלֵינוּ וְעַל כָּל יִשְׂרָאֵל. וְאִמְרוּ אָמֵן:

The casket was brought down into the grave. An endless parade of acquaintances approached it, shoveling soil on it. Berele and Nicolás joined the procession, followed by Elías Fischer, Esther and Enrique, Rosita Shein, Ari and Lorena, and Galia. After her came Beto Brenner, the owner of Joyería La Estrella, a famous jewelry store in the downtown area on Calle Tacuba that carried cheap diamonds and rubies and catered to a lower-middle-class mestizo clientele. As Galia returned to her place, she noticed above the cemetery wall, on her far left, part of a Coca-Cola advertisement. The juxtaposition of the sacred and the profane intrigued her.

Rabbi Sapotnik resumed speaking. "It was said by Ba'al Shem Tov that every Jew, from the abyss of darkness that is life before birth to the abyss of darkness that is life after death, is accompanied by two types of angels: angels of light and angels of darkness. The battle between the two sides takes place at all times. A sin symbolizes a score for the angels of darkness, and a mitzvah is one for the angels of light. When the person dies, the side that scored the most escorts the soul to its final judgment before the Almighty."

He then announced that the shivah was scheduled to start that afternoon in Moishe's apartment on Avenida Horacio 53. Visitors were welcome until Friday—exactly a week after Moishe's death—to pray Shacharit early in the morning, Mincha in the afternoon, and, just before sunset, Ma'ariv. He reminded people to refrain from calling the family by phone at the hours when praying was to take place, in particular between 8:45 and 9:30 A.M. and 6:45 and 7:30 P.M. In order to allow the Tartakovsky family to concentrate on their painful loss, visitors were encouraged to bring kosher food. "It is our duty to make the exodus of Moishe's soul an easy one."

Ari Burak and his wife Lorena moved toward the exit, followed by others. The *levaya* was over by 1:50 P.M.

Galia approached her parents. Her mother subtly pointed in the direction of a female mourner standing almost in the exit. "*La Goye* . . . ," Esther said. "She came too."

"Why not?" Galia replied.

"To a Jewish cemetery?"

"Ah, *Mamá* . . . You still live in a shtetl."

As she was about to leave the cemetery, Galia took one more look at the site where Moishe was put to rest. For a second, she seemed to perceive—magically—a halo emerging from under it. The halo made a pirouette. Was it only a flashing light? An angelic figure perhaps? As she turned around to tell Esther, she realized everyone was already gone.

Suddenly she heard Nicolás's voice from afar. "*Órale,* the chauffeur can't wait for hours." The Volkswagen was a few yards from her, its back door wide open.

First Day

Nicolás took out a set of memorial candles from his suitcase. He then went to the kitchen, where he found an empty wine bottle. He washed it in the sink, dried it, and returned to his room. Galia followed him as he put the items on a table near the wall in the dining room, where they would be visible yet people would not stumble on them.

"What are they for?" she asked.

"Just as the Chevrah Kadishah did at the cemetery, these candles need to be lighted with a bottle of water nearby."

She was puzzled: "I don't get it."

"The soul lives on light and water. By Friday, both will be gone . . ."

"I understand the fact that the wax will ultimately be consumed. But the water?"

"Moishe will drink it," Nicolás responded. He took a glass and filled it with water from the bathroom sink. Galia followed him, amused. "His spirit will need replenishments for the journey."

"Morirse está en hebreo," she replied.

She meant it as a reconfiguration of a famous saying in Spanish, *estar en chino,* to be in Chinese, a language with a graphic system deemed almost undecipherable. If a task— say putting a jigsaw puzzle together—was perceived by someone to be too daunting, the person would say: *El rompecabezas está en chino.* For Galia, though, Chinese and Hebrew were synonymous—foreign, distant, enigmatic.

The apartment was a spacious fifth-floor penthouse at the busy intersection of Avenida Horacio and Calle Hegel. Its aesthetics were pitched firmly in the seventies, even though Moishe moved there in 1989, a few months after Hilda's death. To get to it one needed to take the stairs, which wrapped around the elevator—a small, old-fashioned metallic box with space for a maximum of three people.

"Isn't it ironic that Moishe, a Mexican Jewish patriarch, lived on streets named after a Greek and a German philosopher?" Galia wondered out loud. "No wonder he was so secular."

The elevator door opened and Esther walked in. She hadn't been in Moishe's apartment for months. She carefully studied the place. It looked strange.

She went to the kitchen. *"Hola,* Trini," she said.

"Buenas tardes, señora Esther," the maid responded.

"Don Moishe left us so suddenly."

"*Sí.*"

Galia entered. She asked her mother what kinds of activities Moishe did to keep himself busy.

"I don't know," Esther replied. She thought for a while. "Athletics in the morning, managing his bank accounts at noon, spending time at C.D.I. in the afternoon, poker in the evening."

"Every day?"

"Darling, at seventy, is there a better life?"

"*Mamá*, I mean no offense but don't you think you should know how your father spent his time?"

"Not at all. Do *you* know how I spend my time? I would assume it's none of your business."

"Trini told Rosita Shein that Moishe hardly slept in this apartment. Isn't it true, Trini?"

"Yes, señora Galia."

"Where did he sleep?"

"I don't know. He returned home early in the morning."

"At what time?"

"Three-thirty. Four," Trini responded.

"No wonder everything smells stale," Galia added.

"Maybe he was at *La Goye*'s place? I'm sure he lived with her. Moishe himself used Yiddish to refer to her."

"For you the world is divided in two: the Jews and everyone else. I'm sorry, Trini, but my mother is a bit loony."

Trini looked puzzled. "Are you talking about señora Mabel?"

"Yes," Esther responded.

"They hadn't seen each other for several months."

There was silence. "My father figured out a way to make us all think he was happy," Esther stated.

"Even if he wasn't," Galia added.

Nicolás entered the kitchen to ask for her help to keep a section of the refrigerator kosher. He was about to go shopping for food and wanted to place it in a clean area. Trini opened the fridge and moved items around. Nicolás thanked her and said he would be back soon. He then moved to the living room, placed a pile of yarmulkes on a table where everyone could see them, and took the elevator down to the street.

Galia followed him. As they reached Avenida Horacio, she said: "No need to work that hard, *primo*. The house is forever *treif* . . ."

"It can be purified, though. I'm placing a condolence book in a prominent spot near the entrance door of the apartment. Make sure people write comments in it."

"Why do people need to sit on the floor during shivah?" Galia asked.

"Death humbles us all," Nicolás answered. "It doesn't discriminate between kings and paupers. Also, as Moishe's soul is getting ready to depart, ours become heavier."

"Do you really believe in that crap?"

"Moishe's soul might be trapped in the mirror's reflection," Nicolás preached. "The deceased's spirit lingers on Earth for days before it reaches the 'other side.' It deserves humility. The male members of the family cannot shave."

Galia laughed. "Will the spirit need food too, *primo?*" she pondered. "I'm told a succulent dish of *pescado a la veracruzana* is scheduled to arrive in the apartment before noon. I'm already salivating . . ."

Nicolás was oblivious. Galia laughed again. "What made you become so Orthodox? And to think that in your youth you and your pals took part in a bank robbery, like Bonnie and Clyde. *¡Ay, qué vergüenza!* Tell me, *primo*, does it trouble you not to have served time?"

Nicolás looked annoyed. He hadn't flown in from Ben-Gurion Airport to answer impertinent questions. Nor did he want to engage in fights. Animosity was something from the past. He considered himself lucky to have found the Almighty.

They entered a specialty store. Nicolás searched for salads, sodas, and bread. He read their ingredients carefully. After he paid, the cousins returned to the apartment to find scores of visitors. Most of them congregated in the living room. Galia sat down on an empty pillow near a sofa. She fixed her gaze on the window. Outside it was overcast. "Ay, the city is always gray. Spring, summer, autumn, winter . . . No matter the season, it looks depressed."

Not too far to her right, Elías Fischer reacted to her statement. "That's your perception."

They began a conversation. Fischer was interested in politics. Before coming to the shivah, he watched the news on TV. "Vicente Fox is the favorite in the polls," he said.

Galia asked him about Fox's plan for the future. "It isn't clear," Fischer responded. "People don't seem to care, though. The population is ready for change."

"Is change good?" Galia asked.

"It is the only thing we can be certain about," Fischer responded.

Having placed the kosher food in the refrigerator, Nicolás joined them.

"Have you seen how gray the sky is, *primo*?" she inquired.

"The Almighty likes the color gray," he said. "In fact, He likes every color. Or maybe He is just uninterested in color and attracted to content."

"To content?"

"The Almighty isn't interested in details."

"Are you sure?" she asked. "And do you think He likes Mexicans?"

He turned around in disbelief. "What?"

"I wonder if God—your God, to be precise—likes Mexicans."

"He loves all creatures."

"Ay, Nicolás. You sound like an evangelist!"

The elevator door opened again. And then again. Suddenly, the apartment was packed to capacity. The phone began to ring as well. Relatives from across the globe—Miami, Detroit, Omaha, Amherst, Chicago, and then Buenos Aires, Paris, Johannesburg, and Tel Aviv—called to convey their condolences.

Saturated by the crowd, Galia wandered into the second floor. She found the decor atrocious. There were plenty of souvenirs from trips to Israel (menorahs, jars containing Sinai Desert sand, a poster of the Sea of Galilee, and so on) juxtaposed with yellowish paperbacks (among them *Future Shock* by Alvin Toffler, *The Good Earth* by Pearl S. Buck, *Cosmos* by Carl Sagan, a couple of romances by Danielle Steele translated into Spanish, *The Captain's Verses* by Pablo Neruda, *A Wedding in Brownsville and Other Stories* by Isaac Bashevis Singer, *The One-Handed Pianist* by Ilan Stavans) and an insurmountable array of faded family photographs: Moishe in the Parthenon, Moishe in Yad Vashem, Moishe at the Eiffel Tower, Moishe and Nicolás near the Wailing Wall, Moishe and Berele at the entrance of the leather factory in Calle Bolívar, in the downtown area, Moishe's parents Leibele and Bashe Tartakovsky in Lithuania, Moishe visiting a Jewish cemetery in Belarus . . .

"Pure kitsch," Galia thought to herself.

On a wall she came across a photograph of Hilda at Nicolás's middle school graduation. In it Nicolás looked dramatically different: no beard, no *peyes*, no black suit. Instead, he wore the uniform of Las Chivas soccer team, his sideburns long, his hairstyle making him look like John Lennon in his heyday.

Galia looked for more pictures of Hilda but none were to be found. "A person's memorabilia is an exercise in self-censorship," she concluded.

She descended the staircase again. People were eating and schmoozing. She saw Fischer talking to an elderly gentleman. As she approached them, he introduced her to Zuri Balkoff, Moishe's lawyer. Before they were able to say anything more, Rabbi Sapotnik called upon the men to make a *minyan* and distributed prayer books and yarmulkes. The Amida, part of the Ma'ariv service, was about to begin.

A crowd gathered and moved to the dining room. The rabbi started to sing in Hebrew. Suddenly, the phone rang and Esther picked it up. It was Berele. He told her he was unable to make it today. Tomorrow he would be in the apartment early in the morning. "You should be ashamed! No leisure is allowed during the shivah. People are wondering why you aren't around to mourn your father."

Twenty minutes later, Berele phoned again, this time from his Mercedes Benz. Enrique answered. Berele asked if Nicolás was around.

"He's praying. The Aleinu portion isn't far . . ."

"You should look out the window," Berele added. "Do you see them?"

"What?"

"Come on, look out."

Enrique approached the window.

"Do you see the blue Chevrolet?" Berele asked over the phone.

Through the massive windows, Enrique spotted the automobile his brother-in-law was referring to. It was parked on Calle Hegel.

"Yes, I see it." He moved toward the staircase. He didn't want to bother anyone with his conversation. "I thought it would be better for Nicolás not to be close to the police."

"*¡Idiota!* These aren't policemen. Why involve the police? Obituaries for Moishe are scheduled for the Monday edition of the newspapers *Excélsior* and *El Universal.* Do you know the Feinsods in Guadalajara—Marcel Feinsod?" Berele asked.

"He married Gitele Bronstein."

"His father-in-law, who lives in Monterrey, is a millionaire. He made his money in cement. In any case, Marcel was kidnapped six weeks ago and the family never alerted the police. It would have been worse. Instead, they contracted an Israeli agent who immigrated to Mexico in 1995 and has built a business advising the families of kidnapped victims how to deal with the situation. Marcel Feinsod was kept for fourteen days in a coffin, blindfolded and hand-tied. The kidnappers put earphones on him to keep him isolated. The only sound he could hear the whole time was a loud noise, like the cracking of walnuts. He was only allowed to turn around once a day, when food was brought to him. There was a small bucket near him in case he needed to pee. He was allowed to visit the toilet but twice he soiled himself. For some reason, he was allowed to keep his wedding ring. To count the days—what he thought were days—he moved the ring from one finger to another. After he was set free, he could not tolerate daylight. He's still frightened to go outside. No one in the Feinsod family wants to say anything but I think a ransom of three million dollars was paid. Do you know how much the amount is in pesos?"

"Berele, don't be ridiculous! Do I live on Mars?"

"Almost thirty million pesos . . . You could buy a condo in Miami with that amount."

"And?"

"Marcel Feinsod was finally returned home. He was safe and sound," Berele said.

"I'm sure he had bodyguards."

"You're right, Enrique, although his bodyguards were probably involved in the kidnapping, too."

"*¡Viva México!*"

"What option is there, though?" asked Berele. "Be without bodyguards?"

"You should stop worrying. It's a long time since the robbery. If Nicolás wasn't stopped at customs . . ."

"Enrique, I was a hundred percent sure they wouldn't

stop him at the airport," Berele added. "The Mexican legal system is corrupt. It doesn't keep track of its own deficiencies. Still, the extradition is pending . . . Nicolás shouldn't have come back from Israel."

"It was his choice. After the bank robbery he left Mexico in a hurry. Moishe made the arrangements, you didn't. In fact, you behaved liked a coward. I'm sure Nicolás wanted to be at his grandfather's funeral in order to say thank you."

"Could I have stopped him? My son has his own mind," Berele responded.

"He does, fortunately," Enrique stated.

"As soon as Nicolás confirmed his visit from Israel, I hired the guys in the Chevrolet. The last thing I want is for any of us to be a victim of kidnappers. On the other hand, his plight shouldn't put anyone else at risk. Do you agree? Jews are always an easy target."

"You're paranoid, Berele."

"I'm just being cautious. Please don't mention it to anyone."

"Okay."

"It isn't paranoia, Enrique. Should the police want to arrest Nicolás, the guys in the Chevrolet have been instructed to help."

"How?" asked Enrique.

"Well, I could pretend to be kidnapping him."

"What?"

"I'm kidding, *cuñado,*" Berele said.

As Enrique forced himself to laugh, Esther and Galia showed up. Esther made a sign to him to swiftly conclude the phone conversation.

"My brother's drama belongs to a *telenovela.* Not to this shivah."

"Are you sure there's a difference?" Galia asked.

Second Day

On Monday afternoon, the apartment was packed again. Ari and his father Enrique were sitting together in the studio. Both had taken time off from their respective medical practices. Galia was at their side.

"In my eyes, your *zeide* was a selfish bastard," Enrique, his five o'clock shadow visible already, announced. "Excuse my language and may his memory rest in peace. My own mother, Elsa Burak, eighty-three years old next month, may she live to be one hundred and twenty, lives at the Eishel now. Throughout her life she thoroughly disliked Moishe and Hilda Tartakovsky. They weren't kind to her. Not Hilda when she was married to Moishe, and not Moishe when he became a widower. *Tolerance* is a word I remember invoking often. What do you do with the family? You tolerate it. In Rabbi Sapotnik's sermon at the *levaya,* your *zeide* was portrayed as a saint. This is because death cleanses us from the ugliness we dress ourselves with."

"I'm not sure . . . ," Ari interjected. "Moishe sent me a package by mail every month to St. Louis, Missouri, while I was doing my residency: food, books, photographs, and a fat check. It always arrived on Wednesdays by certified mail."

"Wow."

"I'm sure I mentioned it to you, *Papá,*" Ari added.

"Not that I'm doubting it. It simply didn't register in my mind. I don't believe it registered in your mother's either. In any case, your uncle Bernardo's behavior during the *levaya* was reprehensible. It is also predictable . . ."

As Enrique was talking, Elías Fischer, Rosita Shein, and Zuri Balkoff entered the room. The Buraks immediately shifted their tone and began talking about other matters.

To improvise a different approach to the topic, Galia asked: "When did you last see Moishe, señor Fischer?"

"It was I who was jogging with him at the C.D.I. track, of course. The image of him inert won't disappear from my mind. But he and I spent his last day together. It's a privilege the Almighty offered me, although, in retrospect, I find it eerie—even uncanny—that a person would be given such a privilege. In retrospect it feels as if Moishe indulged in a long farewell before he departed. A couple of weeks ago, we met on Thursday at his favorite spot, Café

La Blanca, not too far from the leather factory, for a suc‐
culent breakfast. He ate *huevos rancheros, pan dulce,* and *café
con leche;* I had *chilaquiles* and *chocolate caliente.* He was as
talkative as ever, although in a fragile mood. He had no
other appointments, he told me. He asked me to walk with
him. He wanted to revisit the places of his childhood. He
took me to the Alameda Central and showed me the bench
where he kissed Hilda for the first time. *'Me le declaré aquí
mismo,'* he said to me. 'We kissed for the first time, then we
shared a cotton candy.' An ice cream vendor was around.
Moishe bought one scoop of lemon sorbet for himself. He
devoured it. His appetite was insatiable that day."

"Did Moishe have diabetes?" Galia asked.

"Not diabetes," Fischer responded.

"Every so often he suffered from bowel irregularities,"
Rosita added. "I once took him to a doctor and they ran
some tests and he was given some medication. That was
several years ago."

"How about a heart condition?" Galia inquired. "Is it
true that once in Houston, a few months ago, Moishe
needed to be hospitalized because of chest pains?"

Rosita smirked. "I never heard of it. Didn't he swim al‐
most every day at the C.D.I. pool?"

"What was he doing in Houston?" Enrique said.

Ari responded, "The last time I saw him, at Baby
Lucy's birth, he told me about it. He said he had been in
Michigan visiting someone. The night before at the hotel

he was uncomfortable. There was some localized pain in the middle of his chest. He pointed to the precise location. He said he felt as if someone was putting pressure there with an index finger. He disregarded it, though. When he woke up next morning, the sensation was the same but he also felt some echoes around the shoulders. Again, he ignored it. On the flight to Houston, a few hours later, he couldn't breathe. He still wasn't sure if it was real or his mind was playing tricks on him. As soon as he landed, he went to see a Mexican Jewish cardiologist friend of mine."

"How did he find him?" Balkoff was curious.

Ari responded: "Moishe called me collect."

"He never called collect," Rosita corrected.

"Perhaps you're right," Ari responded. He thought for a moment. "In any case, I told him to go see Josef Varon. He and I did our residency in St. Louis."

"And?" Enrique wondered.

"When he arrived, Dr. Varon was waiting for him and immediately tested Moishe for all sorts of symptoms. The first results were not conclusive, so more tests were needed. That night *Zeide* spent in the hospital. He had an electrocardiogram, then in the afternoon he underwent a stress test. His physical condition was fine, he was told. By seven P.M. he was released."

"Really?" Rosita was puzzled. "Another acquaintance of mine also did heart tests in Houston. For a day at the hospital he paid twelve thousand dollars."

"Varon and I were in close contact. Two weeks later more tests were carried out," Ari continued. "Moishe was told he needed to go to Rochester, Minnesota, for more studies."

"A world traveler," Enrique stated.

"He didn't go, though," Ari affirmed.

"Why not?" Galia asked.

"I guess he chose not to."

Enrique: "What do you mean?"

"Moishe didn't tell me. In fact, he and I didn't talk again. Some time after he was back from Houston, I called him. Twice he evaded my messages, maybe thrice. I assume he didn't want to go through any treatment."

Galia again: "Why not?"

"Perhaps he was tired . . ." Fischer interceded. "The day we wandered around the downtown area, Moishe was melancholic. It was probably after the tests. He talked of feeling lightheaded. I asked him if he was fine. He said he was okay, but had been experiencing a different kind of symptom."

"How so?" Rosita inquired.

"He said he was loath to seeing himself reflected on surfaces. Before he shaved, he told me, he always let the water run in the sink until it accumulated. He let it stay there for a few seconds before he took out the shaving blade."

"He still shaved the old-fashioned way," Galia commented.

"Moishe told me that he got scared one morning when he couldn't see his face reflected on the water." Fischer stopped momentarily. "He made me promise never to say it to anyone. Moishe said that his inner terror became unbearable the day he again got ready to shave but no reflection of him appeared on the mirror, only a blinding light."

"A halo," Galia added.

"Several days later," Fischer went on, "during our regular Thursday walk, we stopped before the window of a pastry shop. Our reflection was on the window all right, but only I was able to see it." Fischer paused for a few seconds. "'Elías, *querido amigo*, I'm very scared . . . ,' Moishe said to me. 'I feel as if I'm dying already.'"

"Impossible," Enrique stated matter-of-factly.

Fischer went on: "At the Alameda Central, he and I stumbled upon a plaque that read: 'Plaza del Quemadero.' It was the place where heretics were burned at the stake by the Inquisition during colonial times. Mexico had been known as a hotbed of 'Judaizers.' Several famous autos-da-fé took place at the end of the sixteenth century. Moishe became angry. 'I didn't realize the place Hilda and I fell in love had been the site of martyrdom,' he said. He then told me a story. He said that a trusted worker of his at the leather factory, whom he had employed for years, entered his office unexpectedly once. The man had been raised Catholic but a few months earlier had discovered in the closet of his recently deceased mother a set of items that he thought belonged to his boss's faith. He asked Moishe if he would take a look at them, and a few days later the man brought a suitcase that contained a menorah, a Passover wine cup, a prayer shawl, and a set of books in Aramaic. Moishe and the worker talked for an hour. He offered to sell the items, but the worker was offended and said, 'I expected respect from you, señor Moishe. You want to steal these items from me? The Inquisition persecuted my mother's family. I needed guidance from you.' A conversation that started cordially ended in dispute. The worker leaving Moishe's office in dismay made him feel utterly worthless. He tried to look for him but could not bring himself to do it. Moishe told me: 'To this day, Elías, I long for him.'"

"Depressing," Galia stated.

Berele had just arrived in the apartment and suddenly appeared before them. He looked a bit agitated, perhaps because as he had boarded the elevator on his way up, he had come across Trini, who was on her way out to run some errands. Berele forced the maid to stay inside and ride up again. The elevator had barely enough room for a couple of people so no one else was in it. As the door closed, Berele smiled at her and fondled her breast and buttock. She didn't offer any resistance. In fact, it looked as if the encounter wasn't the first of its kind. Others had taken place before. A few seconds later as the door opened onto the fifth floor, he took a brand-new one-thousand-peso bill and placed it between Trini's breasts. Just before the door opened again, he said: "For your little house near the lake of Texcoco." By the time he reached the studio, he looked almost composed again, his sweatpants neat, his hair in place. *"Perdón, mil perdones,"* he said to Balkoff. "I had an urgent to-do at the C.D.I."

Looking at Berele from the stairs leading up to the second floor of the penthouse, Fischer murmured in Yiddish: "Once a *luftmentch* . . ."

Everyone else pretended not to pay any attention to his arrival—with the exception of Esther. She had seen Berele arrive from the living room and followed him as he greeted relatives and acquaintances. She finally cornered him in the studio.

"You've made it, at long last," she said annoyingly. "Aren't you ashamed?"

"Why should I be ashamed?"

"Your father died and you're dressed as if the Olympic Games were about to be inaugurated."

"Esther, for me Moishe died years ago. Plus, I don't need another mother. Save your reprimands for someone else."

Galia was uncomfortable. She left the room. On the second floor, she found Nicolás. He had been praying in the kitchen.

"*Primo,* do you know the word *shivah* refers to a deity in the Vedic Scriptures?"

He responded with a gesture of uninterest.

"The word means 'the pure one.' It is one of the primeval consciousnesses."

"A coincidence, Galia."

"Do you believe in the reincarnation of the soul?"

"Not really. The *Talmud* claims that a single good deed on this Earth is worth an eternal life in the World to Come."

She thought for a second. "So this means there is a World to Come, even if it isn't worth what we go through here?"

"The arrival of the Messiah will reunite all Jews, past, present, and future. Everyone will be transported to Israel."

"And when will he come? Can he show up in the form of a politician, for instance?"

"He will come when all Jews perform at once and simultaneously the six hundred and thirteen principles—the mitzvoth—Maimonides listed for us."

"And they are?"

"Ay, Galia, they go from the belief in one God to the prohibition against incest and the observance of dietary laws."

"Do you know them by heart?"

He hesitated. "I do, yes."

"Which is your favorite principle?"

Nicolás smiled. "I like number six hundred and ten: 'One should not panic and retreat during battle.'"

Galia was amazed. "I didn't know you were a warrior, *primo.*" She opened the refrigerator and looked inside.

"I wish I had a beer."

"No drinking during shivah," Nicolás stated.

She closed the refrigerator, stepped out to the balcony for a minute, and returned. "*Oye,* do you think *Zeide* ever felt Mexican?"

"Who cares? Mexico is a temporary home. Everyone should make aliyah. In fact, Moishe told me in one of his trips to Israel that he was hoping to emigrate."

"Really?"

"I'm not kidding."

"How advanced was he in his plan?"

"I have no idea."

"In other words, it was wishful thinking," Galia stated.

"Maybe . . . In any case, nationalism is a distraction from faith."

She was taken by surprise. "Ay, please don't give me that bullshit again. In Israel, the Orthodox population ignores the quagmire that is the Middle Eastern conflict. They get a free ride, not being forced to enlist in the army."

"We aren't soldiers but scholars."

"Who will defend your country of scholars when no soldiers are left?"

"The army is only for the unfaithful—the perplexed," he added.

"Put your faith aside for a break."

"And who defends Mexican Jews? What kind of army do they have?"

"I didn't think you would be a Zionist diehard."

"I'm not," Nicolás replied.

"Your Almighty protects Mexican Jews, doesn't He?"

Around 5:30 P.M., the telephone rang and Esther answered. It was Mabel Palafox. "I don't want to be intrusive," she gently stated. "Nor do I want to make the family unhappy. Is it all right if I come for a visit?"

Esther appeared speechless while Galia stood by. Then she said: "Yes, please come."

She put the phone down.

"*Mamá,* you were so gentle . . . What happened with the so-called *La Goye?* It was she, wasn't it?"

"Well, the shiksa sounds like a fine lady. She expressed her condolences, said she hoped not to have inconvenienced anyone by attending the funeral at a distance, and wondered if she could stop by to say thank you to the family."

"Thank you?" Galia asked.

"Moishe had not visited her in months. She said: 'But he and I enjoyed beautiful moments together.'"

News of the arrival of *La Goye* put the apartment upside down. "Everyone needs to behave, please," Esther announced.

Half an hour later, the doorbell rang. Trini buzzed the visitor in. Minutes later, Esther and Enrique welcomed a svelte, dark-skinned, fifty-three-year-old *mestiza,* who smiled humbly. Her elegant black dress made her look like an actress.

"I don't believe we know each other. I'm Mabel Palafox."

"Nice to meet you," Esther answered.

Enrique asked if the visitor was hungry.

"No, de verdad. Estoy bien, gracias."

"There is plenty to eat," Esther announced. "After seven days of grieving, the only one not in need of a diet is my father-in-law, may he rest in peace."

Warmly greeting Mabel, Trini brought a plate filled with a variety of delicacies—crystallized fruit, gelatin, *leikach* . . . The atmosphere was relaxed. Still, Esther was anxious. To prevent a disaster, Esther was ready to monopolize Mabel. Although they had never had a tête-à-tête, there was plenty to talk about. Fortunately, Berele hadn't yet descended from his cloud to join the mourners.

For several minutes the conversation was inane. Soon it became intimate. Esther was surprised by how much she liked Mabel.

"Your father was a mensch."

Esther laughed.

"I'm from Mérida, Yucatán. I come from a humble background. As a child I don't remember ever seeing a Jew. They were mentioned in church, usually in ugly terms— the Jew had horns, a pigtail, the Jew used the blood of Christian children to bake the Passover bread . . . Moishe taught me the other side. I loved him dearly. I worked for a partner of his in the leather business. Our romance was the stuff of Hollywood in the fifties—he brought mariachis to my window, serenading me every week; he took me to dinner at elegant restaurants. I won't go into details but the nights we spent in my apartment were rejuvenating. The last couple of years were miserable, though. Moishe was distracted. We took a trip to the Holy Land but he wanted to be away from me most of the time."

"Why?" Esther inquired.

"I asked but was never given a clear-cut answer."

"Did the two of you get tired of each other?"

"Maybe I was his forbidden fruit. Once he was saturated with its flavor, he decided to move on."

Esther added: "And did he ever talk about us to you?"

"All the time," Mabel replied. "In fact, I was the one often persuading him to call you. But he felt uncomfortable. It wasn't his children he was angry at, but himself. I would ask him: What is it that makes you so uncomfortable? Is it the fact that we're together, that you're with me, a non-Jew? Do you think they're offended? At first he was afraid to tell all of you about me. Yes, my presence ignited his unhappiness. My family, mind you, also objected, especially my father . . . But I didn't care. Moishe was so gentile, so honest and generous."

"You don't mean gentile but genteel."

"Yes, *gentil*."

"Who told you about his death?"

"Trini called me."

Esther reflected for a second. "When was the last time you saw each other?"

"Ay, I can't remember. Perhaps last year? I thought that he had found someone else, that I no longer interested him. Then I told myself he might have returned to his family. I looked up your number in an old telephone book of his, but I couldn't make myself call. 'If Moishe wants freedom,' I thought, 'why should I become an obstacle?'"

Galia had sat quietly nearby. It was she who said: "You were not an obstacle but a springboard."

From a loudspeaker on Calle Hegel, Vicente Fox's triumphant voice, sounding self-confident, was heard outside the apartment: "The age of innocence is over."

Third Day

Tuesday was voting day. Unlike previous presidential elections, this time around everybody was eager to make it to the booths. As a result, the crowd at the shivah thinned down until approximately 4:30 P.M.

Nicolás wouldn't vote, of course. A few years back he had relinquished his Mexican passport. Galia wasn't planning on exercising her civic right either. In her case, it was sheer apathy. Why participate in a political farce? Enrique and Esther tried changing her mind but she was skeptical. Hence, throughout the morning the cousins kept pretty much to themselves. Trini was also around but for the most part she kept herself busy cooking a series of dishes Rosita Shein had asked her to prepare.

"It offends me that our religion forbids cremation," Galia said. "When I go, I want to be turned to ashes."

"The Almighty made us and the Almighty will unmake us, too."

Just around then, Elías Fischer entered the place. He was proud to have made his voice as a Mexican be heard. "Will it make a difference?" Galia asked.

"I don't care if it does. It feels good and that's what matters."

"Señor Fischer, I have a question. What if Moishe really wanted to be cremated but didn't have the time to let his family know?"

"To be honest, I don't believe he ever thought about it. You're trying to control his wishes since he's no longer responsible for them."

"What if he visualized his remains spread over the Atlantic Ocean, between the Old World and the New?"

"Galia, that isn't the *zeide* I had," Nicolás replied. "In Israel, he told me that, in spite of the plot he owned in the Ashkenazi cemetery in Mexico, he wished he could be buried in the Mount of Olives."

"Transporting the body would have cost a bundle," Fischer said. "Plus, I never heard him state anything of the sort. Mount of Olives, Shmount of Olives. He wasn't a Zionist. He loved the State of Israel dearly, but never enough to make aliyah. You, too, are putting words in his mouth, Nicolás."

"In the end, it doesn't really matter," Nicolás replied.

"If he didn't state it on paper, it wasn't part of his will. Judaism recognizes that grief is a most difficult feeling. So the mourners are asked to perform mitzvoth—to express their pain, to pray, to share their memories. But Jews are also asked not to indulge in excessive remembrance, for, as Rabbi Yekutiel of Prague said, 'When a man cultivates excessive grief for his dead, he soon finds himself weeping for another dead—himself.'"

Then, astonished, Galia shrieked: "Look, *primo*. The bottle of water . . . It's already half empty." Next were the memorial candles. The flames were steady.

The conversation was interrupted by a wave of visitors entering the apartment. People were inspired by the atmosphere of democracy outside. "Mexico is no longer under a dictatorial regime," someone commented. "A different type of tyranny has descended upon us," Berele announced. "The cacophony of pluralism."

An hour later, Galia, bored with the repetitiveness of the shivah, was looking around inside some drawers in Moishe's office. She came across a bunch of old photographs. One depicted Moishe with some other tourists in Machu Picchu. Other images featured him near the Eiffel Tower, or swimming in the French Riviera, or laden with shopping bags near a department store in Copenhagen . . . She dug further and came across various manila envelopes. The words "Nicolás Tartakovsky: Bar Mitzvah. April 7, 1984" were written on one of them. She opened it.

Inside was an invitation, a couple of photographs, and re-
ceipts and canceled checks. There was also a three-page
handwritten note from Moishe to Berele. Galia read it
attentively. In it Moishe described their long-standing,
troubled relationship, which, as he stated it, began when
Bernardo was still in school. He disapproved of his party
weekends and his rotating girlfriends. "At the time you
needed to land on the ground," Moishe stated. "Your
mother and I looked for alternatives, including sending
you to a military academy. I didn't think anything good
would come out of you . . . and I was right." Galia was intrigued as the tone of the letter became more severe. "If
it had been up to you, Nicolasito wouldn't have had a Bar
Mitzvah. At least I'm thankful you moved aside and let
your mother and me handle the occasion. I'm proud your
mother got to be at the ceremony. The kid needs some direction, just as you did. He cannot grow up to become another Berele."

She was amazed. Clearly, after Berele's default as a
parent, Moishe had assumed the responsibility of Nicolás's
education, not only while Hilda Tartakovsky was alive but
even four years later, after she died. Did it happen too late,
though? After all, not until Nicolás's late teens—once the
robbery took place and he was already in Jerusalem—did
he quiet down. There were several necrologies published in
1988 and a bunch of cards expressing condolence, although
none was from Berele. As Galia's curiosity grew, she took

more items from the drawer and came up with photographs depicting Nicolás, already an Orthodox Jew, with his prayer shawl and a yarmulke, near the Wailing Wall. There were also images of Moishe in Haifa with Nicolás, in Zikhron Ya'akov, near the Sea of Galilee in an unidentified restaurant . . .

Galia put the items back in their respective envelopes. She then opened another drawer. It included real estate contracts, tax returns, used passports and IDs, Nicolás's grade reports from the military academy—showing persistent Cs, Ds, and Fs—and currency from different countries. She came across some LPs from the eighties—one by Barry Manilow, another by the Bee Gees. They had probably belonged to Nicolás. There were records of Mexican music: José Alfredo Jiménez, Los Tigres del Norte, Juan Gabriel . . . She also found one by Rubén Blades. One particular lyric in it, "Desapariciones," had been copied onto a sheet of paper. Galia read the chorus:

> *¿Adónde van los desaparecidos?*
> *Busca en el agua y en los matorrales.*
> *¿Y por qué es que se desaparecen?*
> *Porque no todos somos iguales.*
> *¿Y cuándo vuelve el desaparecido?*
> *Cada vez que lo trae el pensamiento.*
> *¿Cómo se le habla al desaparecido?*
> *Con la emoción apretando por dentro.*

She kept on digging . . . There was a philatelic album. Bizarre stamps from Helvetia, Hawaii, Martinique, Nigeria, and Vietnam. In a separate section, she found early Israeli stamps. One was from 1951, another from 1953. Was it Moishe's? Did he have an interest in collecting? She remembered Esther telling her that as a teenager he had been an avid collector. After a while she came across a container without any identifying marks. She opened it and found it full of newspaper clippings about the robbery and Nicolás's part in it. "Thieves attempt bank robbery. Police make two arrests."

A feeling of envy swept through her heart. Why hadn't Moishe connected with her as he had with Nicolás? With her brother Ari their *zeide* had obviously been closer. Was it because she was a woman? She thought that Mexican Jewish women of Moishe's generation were nothing if not servile. They could educate themselves but in the end the male establishment was the one in charge. Did the family gather at Hilda's shivah with the same keenness? In fact, she didn't remember a big to-do when her *bobe* passed away. She made a mental note to ask her mother if there had been one.

As Galia returned the latest batch of material to the second drawer, she came across a video. It said on the outside: "*¿Adiós?*" She examined it closely but was interrupted by voices outside Moishe's office. She felt like a thief, looking into another person's private life, and instantly replaced the video. She fixed her dress a bit, opened the door, looked around, and wondered if anyone had been spying on her.

By now it was late afternoon. The elevator door opened once more and a mariachi band came into the apartment. Fischer and Nicolás put away their prayer books and proceeded to greet the musicians while Galia followed the conversation while standing in the kitchen. Nicolás picked up the yarmulkes piled on the dining room table and gave one to each of the mariachis to cover their heads.

"My name is Nicasio Hernández. My condolences to the family. Don Moisecito was a dear friend. He hired me numerous times to serenade señora Palafox."

"Don Moishe died on Friday," Nicolás said.

"Yes, I heard the news. We're terribly sad . . . We came to pay tribute to him and to sing to the body."

Ari overheard the conversation from the balcony. Fischer hesitated. "The body was buried Sunday."

"Ay, caramba," responded don Nicasio. "Isn't this a wake?"

"Without the body, though," Fischer answered.

"So can we play for the people, then? Don Moisecito was generous to us . . ."

"Maybe another time."

"How about a short song? Don Moisés taught us to sing in *Yiris.*"

"You mean Yiddish?" Nicolás asked.

"Yes, a *ranchera* song in *Yiris.* Don Moisecito used to pick us up at Plaza Garibaldi. For a while he loved serenading señora Palafox. But then he started coming on his own late at night to listen to the band play."

"Late at night?"

"Moisés Tartakovsky?" Fischer asked.

"*Sí*, señor. He sang with us various *ranchera* songs. Then he taught us to sing in *Yiris*."

The anecdote made those who heard it uncomfortable. "Some other time, *amigo*," Fischer added. He pointed in the direction of the living room. A small crowd was preparing for Ma'ariv service. "Mourners are about to start a religious ritual."

Recognizing their inopportune presence, the mariachis agreed to walk toward the elevator. "Some other time, then," repeated don Nicasio.

Just as the elevator door allowed them in again, Galia joined Ari. He was taking a breather on the balcony. Darkness had descended over the metropolis. "Did you hear what the mariachis said?" Galia said.

"What?" Ari wondered.

"Moishe spent hours at Plaza Garibaldi. Our grandfather becomes more enigmatic as time goes by. Teaching mariachis to sing in Yiddish? I didn't even know he was interested in music."

"Neither did I," Ari replied.

Galia thought for a minute: "I wish I had my movie camera. The shivah would make for an extraordinary movie."

In the living room a few minutes later, Esther, trying

to compose herself from the altercation with Berele, was greeted by an elderly man, Pinchas Barshavsky, almost blind, walking with the help of a cane. He interrogated Esther in Yiddish about her state of mind. Was she okay? Was the family coping well with Moishe Tartakovsky's death? Esther tried to avoid him but Barshavsky began to tell her a story: "*Sabes,* when Hilda, your mother, died, Moishe bought the plot in the cemetery. Do you know I sold it to him? And do you have any idea how much it cost him? Only seventy thousand pesos. That was before the peso became lighter than a feather. For that price, he should have acquired a dozen, don't you think? And would you believe what I saw the other day at Panteón Jardín? I came across an imposing ad: 'Sale. Take advantage: buy two lots for the price of one. Give it to a loved one. They'll never forget you.'"

"Obscene," Esther remarked.

"*Obsceno,* yes. But isn't the whole country moving in that direction? Every day one reads in the paper about someone else being kidnapped. Or else, assassinated. Is this what the end of the P.R.I. is about? And I have another story to tell you," continued the relative. "Do you realize how Moishe got his weekend house near Cuautla? He had done a business deal with some *shmendrik* whose assets were suddenly repossessed by the bank. In compensation, Moishe got the house, but it was in terrible shape, just terrible. He knew it would take a lot of money to fix. Better to sell it and buy one in fine shape, right? But Hilda was in love with the place. And when Hilda liked something, nobody could touch it. Moishe knew it would be next to impossible to persuade her to let go of the house. So what did he do? He woke up in the middle of the night and pretended he had had an awful nightmare. *Sabes,* one of those that wake you up in a sweat. He was inconsolable. Hilda, of course, got scared. She asked him right away to describe the nightmare for her. He did so and in enormous detail. 'Hilda, I saw your mother Shayne, may she rest in peace,' he told your mother. 'You did?' Hilda asked. 'And what did she say?' 'She looked dreadful.' 'Well, she is dead. How else would you want her to look?' Moishe continued: 'She said she had a message. I asked her what it was. "Have you been in the house in Cuautla? You must sell it without delay." "Why?" I inquired. "It is haunted with dybbuks. The previous owner was a murderer. He killed his wife and children."' 'A murderer?' Hilda asked. 'That's what your mother said, may she rest in peace.' 'And how did she find out?' 'Well, that I can't answer, Hilda. Do you think I'm familiar with what haunts the dead?' A few days later, the house in Cuautla was sold at a fair price."

Esther smirked. "That is a delicious story. I'm sorry to tell you, though, that my father, Moishe Tartakovsky, never owned a house near Cuautla."

"Yes, he did."

"He didn't . . ."

"And how do you know?" Barshavsky asked.

"Well, I'm his daughter. That might explain it, don't you think?"

"Esthercita, listen to me. I'm a bit older than you are. Perhaps not by much, but enough to make me see things clearer. In Mexico, nothing is what it seems. Our sense of reality is baroque. And do you know what baroque is? A style allowing you to hide behind your own facade. We're all hypocrites . . . We tell the world something, then behave in the exact opposite way. The Moishe Tartakovsky you knew isn't the one I was acquainted with."

"What was yours like?"

"An escape artist. Do you know I was with him once when, at a business breakfast, a powerful Catholic entrepreneur—whose name shall go unmentioned—told your father, in an indicting voice, that the animosity Jews were a target of was justified because they had killed Jesus Christ? This was an individual your brother was eager to do business with. Do you know how Moishe answered? He wanted the entrepreneur to be his partner, so he conceded the point. Yes, he agreed with the Catholic fellow that Jews deserved the punishment of centuries of anti-Semitism because of their actions in Roman times. And do you know what happened next? He struck a deal to sell thousands of leather jackets in department stores like El Puerto de Liverpool all across the country. A man of principles, eh?"

"Don't speak ill of the dead!"

"Bah, the dead are wiser than we think! The question is always: But is it good for the Jews?"

"Never stop asking it, señor Barshavsky," Esther replied.

"Don't you worry, Esthercita."

Fourth Day

In the living room, Esther was surrounded by a group of her girlfriends: the three Ds, as she referred to them: Dana Frumke, Dina Nashelsker, and Dafna Shweid. The three wore fashionable suits, sophisticated high heels, and ostentatious hairdos. Enrique often joked that the amount spent on their respective wardrobes could go a long way to pay for Mexico's foreign debt.

"I don't know if it's true but rumor has it that Moishe's death was foul play," Dafna announced.

"Who told you?" Esther pondered.

"People are saying that Elías Fischer could have saved him," Dina added.

"Fischer isn't a doctor."

"It doesn't take a specialist to administer mouth-to-mouth resuscitation. Maybe Fischer was into some dirty business."

"The obituary in *El Universal* said your father died at the morgue."

"How is that possible? He would have been rushed to a hospital, not to the morgue."

"Have you found his will?"

"Berele and I are scheduled to meet with his lawyer, *licenciado* Balkoff."

"You'll find out the truth then."

"I believe there must be a full-fledged investigation. Were the paramedics that arrived fully certified? I've heard of a case in Puebla in which a band of thieves arrived in an ambulance. They would only answer calls from wealthy individuals. As soon as they arrived, one would inject morphine into the victim. The victim would be placed on a stretcher and carried away. Of course, the ambulance would never make it to the hospital. They would use debit cards at various ATMs."

"No autopsy was done, right?" Dafna inquired. "The real cause of his death will thus remain unknown."

"Yes, in the end there was an autopsy," Esther answered.

"Oy, how come?" Dana argued. "That isn't good . . ."

"In any case, Moishe lived a full life. Didn't he, Esther? He was a world traveler."

Esther was dismayed. Moishe's death was shaking her to the core. It was good to spend time with Galia, to return to the Polanco apartment, to be with friends. She was getting tired of the innuendos. She also missed her weekly routine—her managing of Enrique's ophthalmology practice, her volunteer job as treasurer of Damas Pioneras . . .

She was an orphan now. Would she be able to cope with that fact? Losing one's parents means that there is no longer anyone in between you and death.

The only one left of her immediate family was Berele. Esther had given up on him a while back. He lacked social skills to such an extreme that in private Enrique nicknamed him *El Cucú*.

"Berele has been a mess since he was a teenager," Dina said.

"Worse than his son Nicolás . . . ," Dafna added.

"*Pobrecita de ti,* Esther. You'll have to deal with the legalities with him, there is no escape. He might be a gambler and womanizer beyond the orbit of the community. Still, he's your only sibling."

"Isn't Nicolás's mother a secretary at the leather factory?"

"You know what, *niñas,* I need to take a nap. I'm tired of the conversation." She excused herself and made her way to the staircase.

On her way to the second floor, she overheard a visitor talking about the Jews in Germany prior to World War II. "They waited too long . . . And do you know what sealed their fate?"

"What?" someone asked.

"Democracy. Adolf Hitler was elected chancellor. In other words, his entrance to power was legitimate."

Esther was agitated. The fact that the presidential

election coincided with Moishe's passing accentuated her uneasiness. She was about to ignore what she had heard when she caught herself replying: "Is Mexico dangerous then? Should we be following our children to the United States?"

Esther didn't wait for a response. She reached the second floor and locked herself in a bedroom.

A full life . . . Did Moishe have a full life? How about her?

Downstairs, on the table at the far end of the dining room, Galia inspected the bottle of water. It was half empty. "Moishe must have lived the last period of his life in thirst," she thought to herself. When she looked at the memorial candles, she realized they were also about to expire. She cried out to Nicolás: "Look, *primo*. Maybe I should start believing in ghosts. *El abuelo se nos está yendo . . .*"

Galia got no answer. She looked around. Nicolás wasn't anywhere nearby. He was upstairs napping on a mattress. "Jet-lagged," he later said apologetically.

Approximately half an hour later, Galia, tired of sitting around, entered the elevator. As the door opened on the ground level, she stumbled upon Elías Fischer. They exchanged a few gentle words. She said she needed to take a walk and out of courtesy asked him if he would come with her.

"Sure . . ."

It was around 3:30 P.M. The street was full of activity.

A couple of restaurants not too far away were crowded with customers. A bus stop a few yards away collected a number of passersby. There were ads at the tops of buildings promoting a new soccer stadium, Tequila Sauza Añejo, and a new line of lingerie. On walls pro-democracy posters lit up the neighborhood. Galia paid attention to one: "In democracy, Mexico is reborn." She and Fischer talked about the spirit of transformation under way in the nation. Her time in New York made her look at things with foreign eyes. "Is it possible that in the near future the president would not be part of the P.R.I.? How could the country be handled without a central figure to make every decision?" She also wanted to know if *el genio* was about to leave the bottle. "My mother thinks dangerous times are approaching . . ."

"I doubt it," Fischer replied.

They found a table in a café. The conversation shifted to Moishe.

"Moishe used to take me downtown, to Avenida Francisco I. Madero, when I was a little girl. Esther and Enrique would be busy so *Zeide* would offer himself. I would hold steadfastly to his left hand as we navigated the busy street corners, talked to a leather merchant here, collected a debt there . . ."

Fischer commented that the neighborhood near Avenida Madero was Moishe's equator. "In the last couple of years, he and I religiously came for breakfast on Thursdays. At times we visited the synagogue on Calle Justo Sierra or the *mikvah* on Calle Jesús María." He said Moishe had first lived in this part of town after arriving from Lithuania. "He was a typical immigrant, hungry and penniless."

"It seems to me, from what I hear, that in the end Moishe was persecuted by his own ghosts," Galia said. "I'm trying to assemble his life together. Why did he abandon Mabel?"

"You're not calling her *La Goye* anymore."

"She's a fine lady," Galia replied.

"Moishe was in love with her. They shared the pleasures of intimacy. After Hilda's departure and ultimate death, he was a fragile man, even though he struggled to give people the impression that he was unbroken. The fact that Mabel Palafox had been a model was important to him. I also don't know what happened to Moishe in the end. He spoke almost nothing about what haunted him. My suspicion is that, with Ari achieving success as a doctor, Nicolás settling in Israel, you in New York, and his relationship with Berele at a standstill, there was little he looked forward to. In our poker games he told me about spending the night out alone in a motel for prostitutes not far from the Palacio de Bellas Artes. I asked him if I could be of help. Again, he said everything was fine, just as he had done when he was overwhelmed by terror that morning after not being able to see his image reflected in the mirror."

After a few minutes, Fischer added: "It took a while for him to finally say something meaningful . . . ," he announced.

"What was it?"

"Your grandfather told me a secret. He said the name of the motel he had stayed in was Hotel Garage."

"Was there a woman with him? Did he pick up a whore in Plaza Garibaldi?"

"I asked the same thing, Galia. He said no, he was alone all the time. He told me he was wide awake. Some time in the morning, though, his eyelids about to close, he heard voices and felt a luminous presence. His heart was beating fast. Suddenly he saw his parents, Leibele and Bashe. They looked youthful and were smiling. The last time he had seen them was in Vilnius, near the Neris River, before he departed for Liverpool. Moishe and his older brother Srulek were packed up, ready to travel to America. They were saying good-bye to their parents, knowing quite well that they might never see each other again. In the visitation they were wearing the exact same clothes."

"It was a dream."

"Maybe."

"Moishe told me that his mother approached him and whispered something in his ear. He couldn't understand the words. He tried to tell her that he never made it to New York."

"Was he meant to go there?"

"An uncle had written to them. He was supposed to wait for them outside Ellis Island. But immigration quotas made it impossible for the ship in which the brothers were sailing to reach New York. It was detained in Cuba and no one was allowed to disembark. By the time Srulek and Moishe docked in Veracruz and found themselves a few days later in Xalapa, they had lost their uncle's address. The fact that they never got in touch with their relative saddened Moishe throughout his life."

"I wish I could talk to him now."

Fischer concluded: "Moishe believed that his mother whispered in his ear that there was no need to look for his uncle anymore, that the uncle had died and was waiting for him in the World to Come."

As nightfall approached, Berele was sitting in the back of the Volkswagen, the chauffeur at the wheel. Esther came out of the building onto Calle Hegel. They exaggerated lukewarm kisses.

"I told Balkoff we would arrive soon," he told his sister.

A while later, Esther inquired: "Did you and Moishe often cross paths at the C.D.I.?"

"Why?"

"I don't know . . . It seems to me you also spend enormous amounts of time in the facilities."

"Once or twice. Each of us found strategies to avoid the other. You know, *hermanita*, the Jewish community is a black hole. With the right intention, one can always lose oneself easily in it."

On the radio, the news hour was announced.

"*Por favor,* bring up the volume," Berele told the chauffeur.

In a low, stable voice, the announcer stated: "It's official: Vicente Fox, the candidate for P.A.N., is Mexico's president-elect. President Ernesto Zedillo will soon recognize him as Mexico's new leader."

"Do you think Mexico without the P.R.I. will be a stable place, Berele?" Esther inquired.

"Do we have a choice?"

"Of course we do."

"What choice do we have?"

"Leave."

"Are you serious?"

Esther failed to answer.

"Would Enrique be able to move his ophthalmology practice? To where—near Galia? She's still young. Are you sure she'll stay in New York? And would you leave your granddaughter Lucy behind? I frankly doubt it. In any event, why would you go? Mexico is a land of plenty."

"I just . . ." Esther decided to change the subject. "You know, I'm uncomfortable talking about Moishe's last will and testament before the shivah concludes."

"It needs to be done," Berele replied. "Otherwise, *La Goye* might run away with everything."

"Mabel Palafox? You're kidding . . . Didn't you know she came to the shivah on Monday? I thought you knew. Obviously, you were behaving like a brat."

"Did she?"

"A pleasant lady. Moishe was no fool."

"What did she say? *Sabes,* I feel awful about *Papá* dying near her."

"They hadn't seen each other for a while, either."

"Why do you say 'either'?" Berele inquired.

"The more people describe their last encounters with Moishe, the clearer it becomes that he spent his last months alone."

"Alone? He had dinner with Elías Fischer on Thursday, the night before he died . . ."

"I don't mean it that way. In spite of being with others, everyone feels he was elusive, distant, not his typical self."

"That isn't altogether bad," Berele responded.

The Volkswagen arrived at Balkoff's *bufete,* as he himself called his law firm. It was located in an exclusive building on Avenida Presidente Masaryk. The secretary let them in. Balkoff asked how the Tartakovskys were coping. He apologized for not making it to the shivah yesterday.

A few minutes later, Berele cut to the point. He asked if Balkoff knew where Moishe's last will was. "I do . . . You won't be happy."

Berele asked why and Balkoff was evasive: "It goes without saying that Moishe went through a difficult period in the end."

"The family did, too," Berele responded. "Ever since

his separation from Hilda and her death. He sold their house in Tecamachalco. Soon after, I took over the factory . . ."

Balkoff talked again. "Early last year, on the anniversary of Hilda's death, he called me. I was in Singapore at the time. My secretary told him I would be back in a few days. She asked if he could wait. 'Of course,' Moishe replied. 'I've waited my entire life for this,' he told her. 'Why couldn't I wait a few more days?' When I finally saw him, he said his life had been about possessing, about building up properties—real estate, automobiles, jewelry . . ."

"Did he own a house in Cuautla?" Esther asked.

"In Cuautla?" Berele pondered.

"One in Cuautla, another one in Acapulco, a third one in Tallahassee, Florida. I believe there was another one in Dallas as well."

"What? That's a huge fortune," Berele interceded.

"It was, indeed."

"How did he manage to become that rich?"

"Moishe invested wisely."

"He didn't leave the fortune to Mabel Palafox, did he?"

"She doesn't know but let's say Moishe left her enough not to have to worry about anything for the rest of her life."

"And the rest?" Berele asked.

"Trini, the maid, was also left a solid amount. The will says the money should be used 'to finish construction of a small villa in Texcoco.' When I returned from overseas, I met with him in this office. He told me he had decided to get rid of every *centavo* he had ever owned, one by one."

"All because of *La Goye*," Berele commented. "Mabel Palafox took control of his assets."

The lawyer listened, then continued: "I doubt it, Berele. We discussed his decision at length. It took fewer than three months to liquidate everything."

"Did he leave anything to the family?"

Balkoff was silent.

"Did he?"

"No."

The lawyer took out a file. He handed it to Berele and Esther. They read it slowly.

"How about the Polanco apartment?"

"It was sold six months ago."

"To whom?"

"A Japanese couple. They're scheduled to move in in May."

"That's just a few months," Esther uttered. "I assume everything must be dismantled by then."

"Something isn't right," Berele argued.

"You bet your life," Balkoff responded. There was a prolonged silence. "You must be thinking that your father was angry at you."

"Yes, I am," Esther said.

"He looked peaceful to me. In fact, I specifically asked

him if he didn't deem it appropriate to leave his assets to his children. He said he had transferred a large amount of money to Nicolás's account in Israel."

"Moishe was attached to Nicolás because he felt guilty," Berele stated.

The lawyer continued: "'Nothing for the rest?' I inquired. 'No,' he answered. 'They've already inherited what was meant for them.'"

Esther was crying.

"I'm afraid there are a couple of things more. Even though I tried to talk him out of it, he made a significant donation to Vicente Fox's campaign. I told him it wasn't money worth spending. We all know that the Church is behind his campaign, as are a number of ultraconservative Catholic groups."

"I can't believe it," Esther commented.

Balkoff made a final point: "And in his last will and testament, after his death Moishe asked to be cremated. He didn't want to leave any physical sign of himself. Obviously, it's too late for that now."

Fifth Day

Barely awake, near the toilet, the faucet wide open, Galia yawned. She stretched her arms and neck. She then uncovered the mirror from behind the mantel. She was half

naked, about to take a shower. A towel was at her side. A
pile of linens, towels, and clothes was on the floor. Suddenly, a powerful light emerging from behind her, a puri-
fying light, blinded her.

"Is it Moishe's soul?" she wondered.

Frightened as she was, she thought of running out and
looking for Nicolás. Instead, she took a deep breath, closed
her eyes, and threw cold water on her face. By the time she
raised her sight again, the light had vanished as magically
as it had appeared. Galia opened the door and walked out,
leaving her bra on the floor.

Minutes later, Nicolás entered the bathroom. He was
about to pee when he saw the brassiere. Its sheer presence
troubled him and he began to tremble. What should he do
next? Shouldn't he return it to his cousin immediately?
Orthodoxy sought ways to placate the instincts. Then he
wondered: What if Galia left it around for me in order to
convey some sort of message? He touched it. He smelled
it. It was soft but the scent wasn't delicate. He quickly
wrapped it up in a towel. In his room, he put the towel inside his suitcase, hiding it under socks and pants, leaving
the top open. Then he went downstairs. A fruit plate was
waiting for him in the refrigerator.

By then Galia was in her room. A photograph placed
near the window sill showed Ari and her as children,
dressed up as cowboys. The image made her nostalgic.

They must have been part of a *purimshpiel* at the Yiddishe Shule. Somehow Moishe's shivah felt like a *shpiel,* too.

While getting dressed, she asked herself what Moishe had been thinking in the last minutes of his life. As his heart wobbled, did it occur to him that death was around the corner? She pulled up her jeans. She looked for her bra. Oops, she had left it in the bathroom. She decided to put a shirt on without it. She would retrieve it as soon as she was finished. Next she pondered Moishe's dreams. What kinds of dreams did he have? She thought to herself that a person's dreams amount to a parallel reality.

Once, when she was an eight-year-old girl, she spent the night at Moishe and Hilda's house. Her grandparents still lived in their house in the Tecamachalco neighborhood. The nightmare she had, brief and decisive, was so powerful, so tremendously frightening, she was still scared after all these years. There was a truck full of relatives. The entire Tartakovsky family was in it—except for Ari, who was nine then. Enrique was in the driver's seat, Esther riding shotgun. The truck was moving at approximately sixty miles an hour. Everyone looked joyful until, without any notice, her brother materialized in the middle of the street. Enrique couldn't make the truck stop in time and Ari was run over, his body wedged under the vehicle. As she turned around to see the remains of her sibling through the rear window, his bloody skull rapidly rolled out from under the truck.

After Galia put facial moisturizer on, she returned to the bathroom to look for her bra. She looked around but couldn't find it. Had she left it hanging on the towel hook, behind the door?

It crossed her mind that Nicolás had been in there after she left. Could he have taken it? Out of curiosity, she knocked on his door. Nobody answered. She pushed it a bit. There were several volumes of the *Talmud* wide open on the floor. The Hebrew letters were minuscule. Did her *primo* wear glasses? He could damage his sight reading such text. As she prepared to leave, her eyes focused on the suitcase. The string of the bra could be seen from in between the folds of the towel. She laughed to herself. "Devotion is another form of blindness," she thought.

Around four in the afternoon, an unshaved Enrique was affectionately talking with a pair of middle-aged identical twins, Rifka and Gitele Yoselevitch. They had been in the same class with Esther at the Yiddishe Shule. In his teens Enrique had dated one of them, Gitele, although he always suspected that Rifka often showed up without notice when her sister was indisposed. However, he was never able to catch them in the act of switching identities.

As Rifka excused herself to visit Trini in the kitchen, Gitele quietly drew closer to Enrique. They had been high school sweethearts at the Yiddishe Shule but in the last few years had only seen each other once, at a circumcision.

Their reencounter at Moishe's *levaya*, then, and the chance to talk about the past, felt pleasant to both and wasn't without sexual electricity. Gitele described for Enrique the plastic surgery she had recently undergone in Dallas: an advanced technique to enhance the breasts, making them at once crisp and plump. "I often think of those late evenings in my parents' home in Tecamachalco. Well, I've brought them back to life . . ."

Meanwhile, in the kitchen Esther and Rifka admired the display of Mexican Jewish delicacies—*pozole, huevos en rabo de mestiza, kneidlech,* gefilte fish with *mole, quesadillas de huitlacoche,* and an array of desserts that included cheesecake, crème brûlée, fruit salad, and *arroz con leche.* They all had been brought by the various mourners and arranged patiently on the table by Trini.

Nicolás came in. "A banquet! Rabbi Ishmael ben Sira said: 'Bewail the dead. Hide not your grief. Do not restrain your mourning by preparing a feast.'"

Esther turned to Rifka: "Look at my nephew the medieval sage!"

Rifka turned around and asked Trini: "*¿Votates el otro día?*" "Si, señora Rifka. I went on Tuesday with señora Shein. She picked me up and taught me how to do it."

"You saw that it wasn't difficult," Rifka added. "I wish all Mexicans did the same, rather than choose muteness."

Rifka and Trini left the room, and Esther and Nicolás were alone. "Are you on speaking terms with your father?"

she asked. "He appears to be incapable of coping with Moishe's death. You should give him a hand."

"I don't know if I should . . . He never once visited me in Israel. Moishe did visit, though. He came over with Mabel."

"I knew he had been to the Middle East, but wasn't sure he had stopped by Jerusalem."

"This is more than three years ago. Altogether they spent three weeks in Israel. I don't think my father ever forgave Moishe for kidnapping me out of Mexico."

"You were out of control, my dear."

"I was, for sure," replied Nicolás. "But my father was paralyzed. Moishe, I think, couldn't stand his son's lack of authority. In a matter of days, I was sent to a kibbutz . . ."

"A deep wound. Berele always saw Moishe as impulsive. He repented and tried to bring you back by all means. But your grandfather made it impossible."

At that point Galia, back from a walk on Avenida Horacio, joined the conversation. Nicolás stood up and, as he fixed his bent-down yarmulke, came next to her. "Have you seen that the candles are gone? And so is the water. A sign that Moishe, too, is ready to say *adiós*."

"The word means 'to God,'" Galia said.

Nicolás continued: "I'm packing my suitcase. I've called American Airlines. I leave tomorrow at two-thirty P.M."

"You're not waiting until the end?"

"Berele believes the Mexican police are keeping a close watch on me. Haven't you noticed the Chevrolet parked outside? It has become the joke of the shivah. He believes the sooner I depart, the better it will be for everyone."

"What do *you* think?"

"I don't care."

"Do you repent?" she wondered.

"For what?"

Galia reiterated: "For what? The theft, of course. Doesn't it bother your conscience?"

"I was a fool . . ."

"Without guidance," Galia said.

A silence followed. "The night I spent under arrest, Moishe arrived at the police station. He told me he loved Mexico too much for a member of his family to wreck his relationship with it. He handed me a one-way ticket to Tel Aviv."

"How long did you stay in the kibbutz?"

"I never made it to a kibbutz. Moishe arranged for an Orthodox friend to pick me up. I lived with him and his wife for several months."

"My father, thus, was involved in your 'conversion,'" Esther stated. "But he wasn't religious. In fact, he disliked religion."

"I'm not as certain as you are about it, *Mamá*," Galia pondered. "In any case, he probably realized that if a military academy wasn't able to put my cousin on the right path, maybe it could be done by a strict regimen."

"I myself chose to become *frum,* Galia," Nicolás claimed. "Nobody asked me to . . ."

Galia smiled: "I know."

Nicolás left the room. He walked up the stairs to the terrace above the second floor. It was the only part of the apartment where one could have a little privacy. Berele was standing by, smoking a cigarette. He saw his son approaching and came close to him.

"I assume you didn't have any problems," the father asked.

"Nope, the electronic ticket was fine. Thanks for arranging it," the son replied.

"There's still a warrant for you. You know that?"

"Yes."

"It didn't deter you from returning to your home country."

"It didn't, *Papá*. I promised Moishe I would come back one day."

"When did you promise him?"

"When he visited me last in Jerusalem."

Berele was quiet. "You surely talked to him more often than I did."

"Things were sour between you."

"You bet they were."

"Will you ever come back to Mexico for good?"

It was Nicolás's time to reflect. "I doubt it. I'm happy where I am. Thanks for asking, though."

"Do you have a girlfriend?"

"Orthodoxy doesn't allow for girlfriends, *Papá*."

"A wife?"

"Maybe one day I will."

"Do you have enough money?"

"Yes, I do."

"How come?"

"You know how come. Moishe set up a trust for me. I live on it."

"Is it true that he sent money to your yeshiva?" Berele asked.

"A large amount. I loved him. He helped me out when I most needed it."

"And I didn't."

"I didn't say that . . . You were busy taking care of the factory."

"It is no more. You know that, don't you?"

"Yes. It mysteriously burnt down . . ."

"Are you implying that I set a match to it?"

"I haven't said anything. I'm just repeating what I've heard."

"When are you flying back?"

"I just arrived, *Papá*. Give me a break, please."

"I'm worried the police will be after you."

"Let me be."

"What? Do you want to go to jail?"

"I don't. But I have to live with the fact that I'm a fugitive. I didn't want it to stop me from being at Moishe's side as his soul moved upward to embrace the Almighty."

"The money stolen from the bank was never found. What happened to it?"

"I assume it's still hidden where we left it."

"Where?"

"Somewhere."

"Shouldn't you return it?"

"What for?"

"Why don't you use it, then?"

"It isn't mine, *Papá*."

"Whose is it?"

"Nobody's."

"The other two kids involved in the robbery are in jail."

"I know."

"They claimed not to know where you hid the booty."

"They're right."

"Doesn't it consume you, Nicolás, to know that only you know where the money is hidden?"

"I've forgotten about it."

Overwhelmed by his son's reticence, Berele walked around the terrace. Nicolás stayed in the same place.

"What if Moishe's soul goes to hell?" Berele asked.

Nicolás was about to deliver an affront but he calmed down. "If so, he will be there to greet us," he answered.

Sixth Day

At noon on Friday, the last day of shivah, the handful of attendees cracked jokes about the presidential results. "Corruption is blind. It recognizes no leadership. Today we're in a beautiful pile of shit with the letters P.R.I. visibly written around it; tomorrow we'll be in one with P.A.N. *La misma mierda aunque revolcada . . .*"

Beto Brenner was tired of the conversation. A week of seeing the same crowd had given him a feeling of saturation. He changed the topic to Hollywood flicks, then to Jewish rituals. "I prefer the ritual of 'no visitation.' A shivah is a morbid and counterintuitive event. It unlocks all kinds of painful emotional floodgates. It is better to avoid any extension of suffering."

The other replied: "Plus, it raises profound questions of memory. Should one share mixed feelings about the deceased? It is better not to utter words in the devil's ear."

At that point Jacobo Feher, a prominent intellectual, closeted homosexual, and lifelong Kehila administrator, as well as the author responsible for a book on the Mexican comedian Cantinflas, entered the room. He expressed his affection for Moishe Tartakovsky, after which he engaged Enrique in a lively conversation.

"Let me ask: At what precise moment did Mexican Jews become traitors? When did they lose contact with the nation that welcomed them with open arms?"

Berele, by now his beard almost fully grown, didn't reply.

Feher continued: "Do we love this country to death? Only as long as it allows us to live in the margins of time, unswept by historical currents. Yes, generations come and go, yet not much changes among us. Or does it?"

At that point, by coincidence, someone on the street screamed: "*¡Viva México!*"

Feher smiled. "*¡Viva!*" he said, without much emotion, adding his voice to the choir.

Rabbi Sapotnik, who came every day in the evening, arrived. A *minyan* was quickly formed. Within a few minutes, he and Nicolás were already reading from the prayer book. Their voices did not always match: Rabbi Sapotnik's delivered the Hebrew words with a slight Argentine accent, whereas Nicolás compressed—maybe even bypassed—a number of syllables. When time for the Shema came, he appeared to reach an unprecedented emotional apex:

שְׁמַע יִשְׂרָאֵל, יְיָ אֱלֹהֵינוּ, יְיָ אֶחָד.

בָּרוּךְ שֵׁם כְּבוֹד מַלְכוּתוֹ לְעוֹלָם וָעֶד.

וְאָהַבְתָּ אֵת יְיָ אֱלֹהֶיךָ, בְּכָל לְבָבְךָ, וּבְכָל נַפְשְׁךָ, וּבְכָל מְאֹדֶךָ.

וְהָיוּ הַדְּבָרִים הָאֵלֶּה, אֲשֶׁר אָנֹכִי מְצַוְּךָ הַיּוֹם, עַל לְבָבֶךָ.

וְשִׁנַּנְתָּם לְבָנֶיךָ, וְדִבַּרְתָּ בָּם,

בְּשִׁבְתְּךָ בְּבֵיתֶךָ, וּבְלֶכְתְּךָ בַדֶּרֶךְ, וּבְשָׁכְבְּךָ וּבְקוּמֶךָ.

וּקְשַׁרְתָּם לְאוֹת עַל יָדֶךָ, וְהָיוּ לְטֹטָפֹת בֵּין עֵינֶיךָ.

וּכְתַבְתָּם עַל מְזֻזוֹת בֵּיתֶךָ וּבִשְׁעָרֶיךָ.

In gratitude, Enrique gave the rabbi an envelope with money. Rabbi Sapotnik went around the living room saying good-bye to everyone. "May Moishe's soul achieve peace. And may it await each of us as our own journey toward the Almighty takes place. In the days of the Messiah, we shall all be together again."

Meanwhile, Nicolás turned to Galia: "It's a prayer dating back to the Second Temple in Jerusalem. It is inspired in a passage from the *Book of Ezekiel,* about a time when the Almighty shall be accepted by everyone. It became part of tradition during the Talmudic period."

Galia looked carefully at her cousin. "I leave in fifteen minutes, *prima,*" Nicolás announced. "It was good to see you after these many years. Now I'm eager to return to Israel. It is my place . . . The Sabbath is celebrated there in a way that is beyond words."

She smiled. "Are you taking my brassiere with you?"

He pretended not to know what she was referring to. "What bra?"

"Nothing . . . ," Galia responded. "Don't worry about it!"

He changed the topic. "Guess how I'm going to the airport?"

"How?"

"In the Chevrolet. I have to stop somewhere on the way."

"To do what?"

"I have something to pick up, something I left behind in 1989."

"What is it?" Galia was curious.

"A souvenir from the past," Nicolás responded.

Trini brought Nicolás's suitcase down and placed it next to the elevator. He said farewell to Enrique and Esther, Elías Fischer, and Trini. Standing in the back, near the staircase, was his father, Bernardo. Nicolás approached him: "*Hasta luego, Papá.*"

"I might visit you in Jerusalem," Berele responded.

"Why not?" Nicolás said.

Galia came closer to them. "As Rabbi Sapotnik put it at the *levaya,* the Messiah will bring us all together. By then I'll have a movie done of a shivah among Mexican Jews. The audience will never see the deceased patriarch. It will only be able to visualize him through the sum of contradictory comments expressed by the mourners through the seven-day mourning period."

Nicolás picked up the suitcase and proceeded toward the elevator. Galia kissed him on the cheek. He reacted uncomfortably but smiled in the end.

It was afternoon. Avenida Horacio felt joyful outside. People were doing their shopping before the weekend. Only a few attendees were still in the apartment. Shortly before sunset, the remaining family members would be gathering their ripped shirts, ties, and other clothes used since the *k'riah* was performed at the funeral, collecting them all in a single bag, taking a walk together around the block, and throwing them away in the garbage, a sign that the weeklong mourning period that was concluding with the Sabbath as the seventh day had come to an end. Berele and Esther, far more peaceful than ever before, sat together in the dining room. Esther took the condolences book and began to read it. Ari, like Berele visibly bearded, and his wife Lorena were nearby, as was Galia. The pages were filled with handwritten messages, ranging from a couple of lines to a couple of hefty paragraphs, depicting Moishe in a myriad of ways. The three readers were surprised by the polarizing nature of the statements. Expressions like "affectionate" and "dignified" contrasted with "volcanic emotions" and "unforgiving." One message claimed: "Memory is merciful. It emphasizes the positive." Another one stated: "Let old feuds be forgotten. Children should not pay for the sins of their parents."

Abruptly, Galia asked each of the close relatives and intimate friends to stay around. "You're in for a surprise . . ."

"What kind of surprise?" Ari asked.

"A message from Moishe. A message for us all."

She led everyone to Moishe's office, near the staircase, behind the living room. Once everyone found a place to sit and relax, Galia turned the TV on and placed a cassette into the video recorder under the set. On the screen an amateur film—a poorly lit interior, spacious, looking like an auditorium—began to unfold. At first the lens wavered nervously but the image eventually settled down. Someone was holding the camera while walking around. After a while it became clear that it was Congregación Beit Yitzhak, Moishe's synagogue. It was the sanctum sanctorum, although the place was absolutely empty. In fact, it looked haunted. Judging by the light filtering through the windows, the time could have been the early hours of the morning.

The tape was interrupted. The entire screen went black first, then a scene became clear: the camera was capturing President Zedillo as he greeted members of his cabinet. A newscaster's voice quoted the leader: "'. . . call it a new life,' *El Presidente* said. 'Even though the P.R.I. didn't win the election, it doesn't mean our mission is over. There might not be reincarnation in life, but there is reincarnation in politics. In our country, the past is never buried. The P.R.I. knows that . . .'"

"Is something wrong?" Berele asked, but before Galia stood up to fix the TV the video image restored itself.

"It's a self-made video," Ari said.

Moishe's face was now in a close-up. He was wearing a sombrero. He uttered something in Yiddish.

"What did he say?" Ari wondered.

Fischer added: "He's about to sing like a mariachi."

Moishe made a slight movement. His well-rounded belly, just like a *sandía,* became visible. A melody could be heard from a distance. After several beats, he started singing in Yiddish. Berele laughed. "His key is atrocious . . ." Then Moishe switched to Spanish:

Probablemente ya de mí te has olvidado,

y sin embargo yo te seguiré esperando.

No me he querido ir para ver si algún día

que tú quieras volver me encuentres todavía.

While her *zeide* smiled and again the image broke off, Galia announced swiftly: "A song by Juan Gabriel. I found this video in one of Moishe's drawers. It's his valedictory speech."

Again, the narrative was interrupted for a few seconds. Finally, Moishe showed up again on camera. This time he was sitting near the bimah. He began to talk slowly, as if meticulously dictating each syllable

". . . a man doesn't have a chance to withdraw from the public. Yet there comes a moment when one recognizes that the space we take on this Earth—the hole we inhabit day in and day out—is ceasing to be ours. How long will it take for us to vanish, to become *un fantasma*?"

He took a deep breath. "My seventieth birthday is today. Am I happy? I've decided not to spend it with anybody but myself. A man's worth is the sum of the seeds he's spread around. Mine are dispersed all over the globe. I feel shattered, diminished by each of these departures, these subtractions. Mexico has been extraordinarily generous to me and to thousands of other Jewish immigrants. Have we been equally generous to Mexico? I'm not sure . . ."

Slowly, the image on the TV again became blurry. The

sounds diminished slowly, then vanished altogether. Viewers could only see emptiness.

"Can someone fix it?" Berele asked.

Galia tried unsuccessfully at first. When she was about to give up, Moishe's face on the TV screen returned for an instant. He was smiling—sarcastically. And then, suddenly, a loud hiccup was heard. At that point Galia had the sense that she was witnessing yet another flashing light, like the ones she had seen before. Perhaps it was even an angelic figure, dancing alone in the synagogue, against a dark background. As unexpectedly as the face on the screen returned, it disappeared once and for all.

Elías Fischer let out an expression of frustration: "¡Ay, cabrón!"

Not spoken in language, but in looks
More legible than printed books.

Henry Wadsworth Longfellow, *The Hanging of the Crane*, 1874

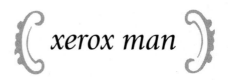

My share in the explosive case of the so-called Xerox Man, as the New York tabloids delighted in describing Reuben Staflovitch shortly after his well-publicized arrest and as the *Harper's* profile reiterated, is too small: It amounts to only fifteen minutes of conversation, of which, unfortunately, I have an all-too-loose recollection.

I first heard of him at Foxy Copies, a small photocopy shop right next to the prewar apartment building where I spent some of my best Manhattan years. The shop's owner was a generous man in his midfifties by the name of Morris. Morris attended his customers with a kind of courtesy and unpretentiousness out of fashion in the city at the time.

I used to visit Foxy Copies almost daily as my duties required material to be Xeroxed and faxed on a regular basis. I refused to have my home invaded by technological equipment, so Morris, for a non-astronomical fee, did the job for me.

He always received me with open arms. If time permitted, he would invite me to schmooze for a little while at his desk behind one of the big photocopy machines. We would discuss the latest Yankee game or that week's Washington scandal. He would then process my documents as if they were his own. He had read one of my pieces once in a trade magazine and prided himself on having what he called "a distinguished list of clients," among which he included me. "You will make me famous one day," he often said.

In one of our conversations I asked Morris, just to be a nuisance, if he ever felt curiosity about his customers and the stuff they photocopied.

"Why should I?" he answered quickly, but then lowered his defenses. "You want me to really answer your question? Then come with me," and we walked together toward a back room with a huge closet, which Morris opened right away. In front of me I saw a stack of disorganized paper.

"In Brooklyn," he said, "an old teacher of mine used to like strange words. When I bought Foxy Copies one of these words came back to me: *paralipomena*. It means remnants that still have some value. What you see here are piles of Xeroxes clients leave behind or throw away."

The sight reminded me of a *genizah*, the annex in every synagogue, usually behind the Ark, where old prayer books accumulate. Disposable Jewish books cannot be thrown away because they might contain the name of God, which can fall into the wrong hands and be desecrated. So these books are stored until the *genizah* gets too crowded, at which point someone, usually an elder, buries the books in the backyard.

"A *genizah* of sorts, isn't it?" I said.

"Yes," Morris answered, "except that a special company comes once every three months or so to pick this stuff up. I hate not to see it properly recycled."

I browsed through the Xeroxes.

"Trash, really," Morris said. "Most of it is in plain English. Except for the remains left behind by Mr. Staflovitch," and as he uttered the name, he pointed to a lower pile. I looked at it closely and its pages appeared to me to be in ancient Semitic languages.

Morris didn't like to talk about his clients but deep inside all New Yorkers are indiscreet and he was too. So he told me that Reuben Staflovitch—yes, as I recall, he used the complete name for the first time at that point—was by far the most taciturn. He described him as well built, of average height, always dressed in a black suit, white shirt, and unpolished moccasins, with an unruly beard and his trademark sky-blue Humphrey Bogart hat. "He comes in with a black doctor's bag about once every two to three weeks," Morris added, "usually at closing time, around six-thirty P.M. He asks to have a Xerox machine all for himself. With extreme meticulousness, he proceeds to take out from the doctor's bag an antiquarian volume, which takes him between thirty and forty minutes to photocopy. Then he restores it to the doctor's bag, wraps the Xeroxed material in plastic, pays at the register, and leaves. Few words are uttered, no human contact is made. He leaves in the exact same way as he arrives: in absolute silence."

I remember talking with Morris about other topics that day, but Staflovitch was the only one who truly captured my imagination. "You know," Morris continued, "it is amazing to watch him do his job. His photocopying is flawless; not a single page is wasted. But just after he finishes, he puts his fingers into the pile and takes out a single copy—only one—and throws it away. Why he does this I have no idea. I never dared to ask. But I save the excluded page out of pity."

I extracted the top page in Staflovitch's pile from the closet. "Can I take it with me?"

"You bet," Morris replied.

That night, in my solitude, I deciphered it: it came from a Latin translation of Maimonides' *Guide for the Perplexed*.

Not long afterward, while on Broadway, I saw Staflovitch himself. Morris's description was impeccable. Except for the Humphrey Bogart hat, he looked as unemblematic as I had imagined him: a nondescript Orthodox Jew just like the ones on Delancey Street. He walked quickly and nervously, with his doctor's bag on his right side. A hunch made me follow him. He headed uptown toward the 96th

Street subway station but continued for many more blocks—almost thirty—until he reached the doorsteps of the Jewish Theological Seminary, where, crossing through the iron gate, he disappeared from sight. I waited for a few minutes and saw him reappear, walk uptown again, this time to Columbus Avenue, and disappear once and for all into an apartment building. "This must be his home," I told myself. I felt anguished, though, wishing that I had come face-to-face with him. I was puzzled by his mysterious identity: Was he married? Did he live alone? How did he support himself? And why did he copy old books so religiously?

When I next saw Morris, I mentioned my pursuit. "I'm feeling guilty now," he confessed. "You might be after a man with no soul."

My fifteen-minute conversation with Staflovitch occurred about a month later, as I was leaving Columbia University after a day of heavy teaching. He was entering the subway station at 116th Street. By chance the two of us descended the staircase together. I turned around pretending to be dumbstruck by the coincidence and said: "I've seen you before, haven't I? Aren't you a Foxy Copies customer?"

His reply was evasive. "Well, not really. I don't like the neighborhood . . . I mean, why? Have you seen me at the shop?"

I instantaneously noticed his heavy Hispanic accent, which the media, especially the TV, later picked on.

"Are you from Argentina?"

"Why do you care?"

"Well, I am a Mexican Jew myself."

"Really? I didn't know there were any. Or else . . ."

Wanting clearly to avoid me, Staflovitch took out a token and went through the turnstile. I didn't have one myself, so I had to stand in line, which delayed me. But I caught up with him after I descended to the train tracks. He was as close to the end of the platform as possible. The train was slow in coming and I wasn't intimidated by his reluctance to speak, so I approached him again. "I see you're in the business of Xeroxing old documents . . ."

"How do you know?"

I don't remember the exact exchange that followed but in the next few minutes Staflovitch explained to me the sum total of his theological views, the same ones expounded to various reporters after he got caught. What I do remember is feeling a sudden, absolute torrent of ideas descending on me without mercy. Something along the lines that the world in which we live—or, better, in which we've been forced to live—is a Xerox of a lost original. Nothing in it is authentic; everything is a copy of a copy. He also said that we're governed by sheer randomness and that God is a madman with no interest in authenticity.

I think I asked him what had brought him to Manhattan, to which he replied: "This is the capital of the twentieth century. Jewish memory is stored in this city.

But the way it has been stored is offensive and inhuman and needs to be corrected right away . . ." The word *inhuman* stuck in my mind. Staflovitch had clearly emphasized it, as if wanting me to savor its meaning for a long time.

"I have a mission," he concluded. "To serve as a conduit in the production of a masterpiece that shall truly reflect the inextricable ways of God's mind."

"You're an Upper West–sider, aren't you?" I asked him. "The other day I saw you on the premises of the Jewish Theological Seminary."

But by that point he had no more patience left and began to shriek: "I don't want to talk to you . . . Leave me alone. Nothing to say, I've nothing to say."

I took a step back and just then, by a bizarre synchronicity, the local train arrived. As I boarded it, I saw Staflovitch turn around and move in the opposite direction, toward the station's exit.

A week later the tabloid headlines read "Copycat Nightmare" and "Xerox Man: An Authentic Thief," and the *New York Times* carried the scandalous news about Staflovitch on its front page. He had been put under arrest on charges of robbery and destruction of a large array of invaluable Jewish rare books.

Apparently he had managed to steal, by means of extremely clever devices, some three hundred precious volumes—among them editions of Bahya ibn Paquda's *Sefer Hobot ha-Lebabot* and a generous portion of the Babylonian *Talmud,* an inscribed version of Spinoza's *Tractatus Theologico-Politicus* published in Amsterdam, and an illu-minated *Haggadah* printed in Egypt—all from private col-lections at renowned universities such as Yale, Yeshiva, Columbia, and Princeton. His sole objective, so the re-porters claimed at first, was to possess the rarest of Judaica, only to destroy the items in the most dramatic of ways: by burning them at dawn inside tin garbage cans along River-side Park. But he only destroyed the literature after photo-copying it in full. "Mr. Staflovitch is a Xerox freak," an officer was quoted as saying. "Replicas are his sole objects of adoration."

His personal odyssey slowly emerged. He had been raised in Buenos Aires in a strict Orthodox environment. At the time of his arrest his father was a famous Hasidic rabbi in Jerusalem with whom he had had frequent clashes, mainly dealing with the nature of God and the role of the Jews in the secular world. In his adolescence Staflovitch became convinced that the ownership of antique Jewish books by non-Orthodox institutions was a wrong in des-perate need of correction. But his obsession had less to do with a transfer of ownership than with a sophisticated the-ory of chaos, which he picked up while at Berkeley in a brief stint of rebellion in the early 1980s. "Disorder for him is the true order," the prison psychologist said, and added: "Ironically, he ceased to move among Orthodox Jews long ago. He is convinced God doesn't actually rule the universe, He simply lets it move in a free-for-all cadence. And humans, in emulation of the divinity, ought to replicate that cadence."

When the police inspected his Columbus Avenue apartment, they found large boxes containing photo-copies. These boxes had not been catalogued either by title or by number; they were simply dumped haphazardly, al-though the photocopies themselves were never actually mixed.

Staflovitch's case prompted a heated debate on issues of copyright and library borrowing systems. It also gener-ated animosity against Orthodox Jews unwilling to be part of modernity.

"Remarkable as it is," Morris told me when I saw him at Foxy Copies after the hoopla quieted down somewhat, "the police never came to me. I assume Staflovitch, in or-der to avoid suspicion, must have enlisted the services of various photocopy shops. I surely never saw him Xerox more than a dozen books out of the three hundred hidden in his apartment."

Morris and I continued to talk about his most famous client, but the more I reflected on the entire affair, the less I felt close to its essence. I regularly visualized Staflovitch in his prison cell, alone but not lonely, wondering to him-self what had been done to his copy collection.

It wasn't until the *Harper's* profile appeared, a couple of months later, that a more complete picture emerged—in

my eyes, at least. Its author was the only one allowed to interview Staflovitch in person on a couple of occasions and
he unearthed bits of information about his past no one else
had reckoned with. For instance, his Argentine roots and
his New York connection. "I hated my Orthodox Jewish
education in Buenos Aires," Staflovitch told him. "Everything in it was derivative. The Spanish-speaking Americas
are pure imitation. They strive to be like Europe, like the
United States, but never will be . . ." And about New York
he said:

> I supported myself with the bequest I got after my
> mother's death. I always thought this city to be the
> one closest to God, not because it is more authen-
> tic—which it isn't, obviously—but because no other
> metropolis on the globe comes even close in the
> amount of photocopying done regularly. Millions
> and millions of copies are made daily in Manhattan.
> But everything else—architecture, the arts, litera-
> ture—is an imitation too, albeit a concealed one.
> Unlike the Americas, New York doesn't strive to be
> like any other place. It simply mimics itself. Therein
> lies its true originality.

Toward the end of the profile, the author allows Staflovitch
a candid moment as he asks him about "his mission," and

reading this portion, I suddenly remembered that it was about his mission that he talked to me most eloquently at the subway station.

"Did the police ever notice that the Xerox boxes in my apartment are all incomplete?" he wondered. "Have they checked each package to see that they are all missing a single page . . .?"

"Did you eliminate that single page?" he is asked.

"Yes, of course. I did it to leave behind a clearer, more convincing picture of our universe, always striving toward completion but never actually attaining it."

"And what did you do with those missing pages?"

"Ah, therein lies the secret . . . My dream was to serve as a conduit in the production of a masterpiece that would truly reflect the inextricable ways of God's mind—a random book, arbitrarily made of pages of other books. But this is a doomed, unattainable task, of course, and thus I left these extricated pages in the trash bins of the photocopy shops I frequented."

When I read this line, I immediately thought of Morris's *genizah* and about how Staflovitch's mission was not about replicating but about creating. I quickly ran downstairs to Foxy Copies. Morris surely must have been the only savvy shop owner to rescue the removed copies. I still had the Maimonides page with me but I desperately wanted to put my hands on the remaining pile of documents, to study them, to grasp the chaos about which Staflovitch spoke so highly. "Paralipomena: This is the legacy the Xerox Man has left me with," I told myself.

Morris wasn't around but one of his employees told me, as I explained my purpose, that the recycling company had come to clear the backroom closet just a couple of days before.

about the author

Ilan Stavans is the Lewis-Sebring Professor in Latin American and Latino Culture and the Five College Fortieth Anniversary Professor at Amherst College.